Henry

Leann Austin

L. Austin Publishing

New York

Leann Austin/L. Austin Publishing

Book Layout © 2017 BookDesignTemplates.com
Cover Design by Sam_designs1

Finding Henry Leann Austin. -- 1st ed.
ISBN 9781659071665

Dedication

To all the brave warriors who survived abusive
husbands and boyfriends.

And to the ones who didn't.

Endorsement

"Emelia Berggren is the kind of everyday girl that makes Finding Henry powerful in its chilling relatability. The author's recreation of a retro 1980's setting and her authentic portrayal of an often misunderstood personality disorder make this not just a compelling read, but an important cautionary tale. A must-read for every girl who gives too much, and asks too little."

~Kathleen L. Maher, Genesis award-winning author of Sons of the Shenandoah Series

CONTENTS

The Pendant

"You will be making a choice between two young men." The crazy fortune teller held my hands in hers. She eyeballed me to the point of discomfort. "Yes. I see one with hair like the golden sun." She closed her eyes, contemplative perhaps.

Why did I let Kelli-Anne talk me into this craziness? A fortune teller at the Gala Days sideshow. Yeah. This wasn't gonna be good.

"And one with raven black hair." Her voice reminded me of a giddy girl on the Ed Sullivan show during the first Beatles performance in the states. "You will choose him."

She brought me back to where I sat in a colorful tapestry chair, in a humid hot tent, a gazing ball on the table between us.

"Huh?"

She opened her cerulean eyes and stared into mine. "Have you not listened to anything I have spoken to you?"

I nodded, but thought about the five dollars I'd wasted on a five minute guessing game.

"The man with raven hair. He is the one you will choose. Must choose." She squeezed my hands with her clammy, boney ones and smiled, her lips deep red over what teeth she had left.

My mind calculated her prediction and it didn't compute. Jasper had golden hair, er, blond hair. I pinched my thigh with my free hand. *Do not talk like this gypsy woman*, I scolded myself. There were no dark "raven" hair men in my life. I was a one man kinda girl.

"Thank you. I'll remember what you told me." Emelia didn't remember. And she would remember when it was too late.

"Here. Wait." The scrawny psychic stood and went to a sea chest covered with a burgundy and gold tapestry. It creaked like my grandma's knees when she walked the stairs. She delved inside and rattled the contents of the chest.

I inched my way backwards towards the tent entrance. The gypsy fortune teller didn't turn around. "You wait. I have something for you. You not listen. You may need this." She stood, one hand on her mid back. In her other hand dangled a gold chain with a pendant.

"It's fine. Really. I don't have any more money." I didn't need a cursed object around my neck.

"No charge. I see you have a good soul. But good souls are magnets for evil."

I swallowed hard at the lump that rose in my throat.

"Our lives cross paths with many others. Some good, we no see. Some bad, we blind to." She shoved the pendant into my hand and closed my fingers firmly around it. I opened them to see what I now held and prayed it didn't carry any bad juju with it.

"What is this?" I twirled the gold filigree pendant. "What are the words here?"

She smiled. "The cycle ends where it begins."

"Okayyy."

"It is Latin. That is what it says roughly." She shrugged her hunched shoulders.

"And? Why do I need this?"

"You have many choices in life. But so young. You will have a difficult choice. One between your heart and your head." She tapped her kerchief clad head.

"I don't need..." I tried to put it into her hand but she pulled away.

"It belongs to you now. It will only respond to your touch."

God help me! Where was Kelli-Anne?

"When you realize you have come to the dead end, of where the wrong choice was made, you can choose to go back to the beginning."

"Of what?" I rubbed my sweaty palms on the legs of my jeans.

"Only you will know the answer to that. And it will take you there."

"Like a time portal?"

"Something like that. Remember, once you use it, it cannot be undone. Only once back to the beginning of the wrong path, but always a way home."

I opened my mouth to argue, tried to drop the thing on her table, but she shoved me towards the tent entrance. "You go. I see more people now."

I stumbled out of the tent and into Kelli-Anne.

"Whoa. Walk much?" Kelli-Anne grabbed the rope anchored to the tent to regain her balance.

"No. That old fortune teller pushed me." I regained my footing and ran a hand through my hair.

"What fortune teller?" Kelli-Anne looked behind me.

"Duh. The one you coerced me to see." I hitched my thumb over my shoulder.

"She's over by the elephants." Kelli-Anne pointed across the midway to a hand painted sign that read *'Madame McMurdy - Fortunes told here.'*

"But, I just talked to her. In here." I opened the tent flap I'd been shoved through; Kelli-Anne peeked over my shoulder.

"You're crazy." Kelli-Anne walked off towards the Tilt-a-Whirl.

Was I? Because the only items inside the tent were packing crates, sacks of peanuts, and an empty table with two burgundy, tapestry chairs.

Yet the pendant in my hands was quite real.

2

Photograph

"She really said that?" Henry tossed a rock into the metal bucket.

"Yeah. Like, what a waste of five dollars." I tossed a stone at the bucket and missed. "Lame. How are you so good at this and I'm so bad?"

"I play on the basketball team." He tossed another rock from my front porch steps and sunk it.

"Yeah, but...okay, good point."

Henry's walk home from school took him past my house and if I was on the porch, writing in my notebook, he'd stop and we'd sit on the steps and throw stones at the metal garden bucket. I don't know how it started. Either he needed help with an essay or it was the day my dad left and I'd been crying on the porch swing. They happened about the same time. However it happened, I found our ritual relaxing.

"Anyways, this gypsy gave you a cursed object? Did you throw it away? Better, did you burn it?" Henry juggled the stones that remained in his hands.

I slid my hand into my pocket and retrieved the pendant. I held it out for Henry to see.

"It doesn't look so bad. Let me see it." He held out his hand.

I handed it to him and he flipped it over a few times. "This is cool." He fingered the filigree and engraved writing, and tried to spin it. It didn't move. "It's broken."

"It worked when she gave it to me. Let me see it again." I held it and moved the pendant inside of its delicate gold circle. "See." I handed it back to him and again he failed to make it move. "Well, the fortune teller said it would only work for me anyways." I laughed.

"What does it do?" He placed it gently in my palm. He pulled his hand away and grazed my fingertips.

"I don't know. The woman talked in riddles." I shoved it back into my pocket.

"Yet, you're keeping it?" He raised an eyebrow at me.

"Well, yeah. I want something for my five dollars. Besides, it holds a memory. And a reminder I should never go to a gypsy fortune teller again." I laughed.

"And she told you to choose the boy with dark hair and not Fabio."

I pushed him and he toppled off the top step. "Hey! What'd ya do that for?"

"For being a dork."

He righted himself, and brushed his hand through his shaggy, medium length brown hair. "I have dark hair."

"So do half the guys in school."

"Hmm." He tossed another pebble and missed the target.

"Ooh. First time for everything." I teased.

"What?" He looked confused.

"I've never seen you miss." I pointed at the bucket.

"Probably dizzy from being pushed off the porch." He nudged me with his shoulder.

I nudged him back. "Naw. Anyways, this gypsy lady must have seen my wallet on the table. She had me close my eyes and probably flipped through the photos. She must have seen my picture of Jasper with his arm around me."

"Maybe." He shrugged and tossed another pebble, which failed to land in the bucket.

"C'mon. You're not buying into this are you? Besides, chances are good I'd know a blond and a brunette. Heck, she could have tossed in a carrot-top for good measure. Although, that's less likely. I have a picture of us in my wallet too." I pulled the slim, red wallet from my back pocket and flipped through the plastic photo insert. I held up a photo of Henry and me sitting on the porch swing. It was the day my little sisters wanted to try out their new face painting kit. Henry and I played along, although I was surprised Henry had let nine year-old Andrea paint him as a Saint Bernard. I was glad I hadn't been the only one whose face was defiled.

Henry looked at the photo and laughed. "You told me you burned it." He reached for my wallet. I hid it behind my back. "Never! Blackmail forever!"

"You are a brat, Emelia Berggren." He reached behind me for the wallet. I slid it into my back pocket and held my hands forward. "No photo. I made it disappear."

Henry reached around my waist with both hands. His long arms encircled me.

"Hey!" I pushed against his chest.

"Where did it go? That picture has to go." He continued to reach behind my back.

"Damn it, Henry. It's in my back pocket. On my butt. Don't..."

He fumbled for my pocket.

"Not cool! Get your hands off my butt." I tried to push him away, but his strength was greater than mine.

"I'm not touching...*that*." Face flushed, he pulled his hand away. He lost his balance, toppled forward, and took me with him. He braced himself above me.

His face was inches from mine, but he didn't move. His Hershey brown eyes stared at me. He swept my bangs away from my forehead gently. So. Gently.

Goosebumps prickled my arms. My breath hitched, kind of like small, repetitive hiccups. That was new for me.

"Sorry." Henry moved away. "I lost my balance."

I swallowed the dry spot away at the back of my throat. "That's okay." My voice cracked. "Just don't do it again." I lightly punched his arm.

"S'up guys?" A car door slammed and I turned to see Jasper. He was headed up my walk at a determined gait. His blue Chevy Nova had never made a sound when it pulled up. The front end was scrunched from a fender-bender. Jasper had secured it shut with a bungee strap. The engine of his classic car was still as quiet as the inside of a funeral home.

"Do not mention the fortune teller," I whispered in Henry's ear. My heart pounded against my ribs. "He doesn't like them."

"Yo. Jasper. Your '*girlfriend*' is blackmailing me." Henry sounded less than irritated.

Nice save. I let out a whoosh of air. If Jasper had seen us goofing around he'd be mad I'd behaved so childishly, but he wouldn't mention it until later when we were alone.

"Oh yeah? What's she got on you?" He hopped onto the steps and glared down at me, still lying flat on the porch. He held out his hand. "What are you doing down there?"

I kept my gaze on Jasper. I tried to read him. Playful mood or jealous? He always accused me of having a thing with Henry, which was absurd. We'd been friends since freshman year, and all we'd ever done was sit on my porch and toss pebbles or work on homework. We'd never walked home together from school and I'd never been to his house.

"I lost my balance trying to keep my wallet from Henry." My voice cracked.

He lifted me to my feet. "Let me see it." His tone made me jump.

"What?" I swallowed.

"What you have to blackmail Henry here with." He extended his hand, his eyes dark.

I laughed, trying to lighten the mood. "It's just a silly picture. I was only teasing him about it."

"Let me see it so I can be in on the joke." He wiggled his fingers on his still extended large hand.

"It's okay man." Henry's voice rasped. "It's nothing I'm worried about." He clenched his hands at his sides.

"Emelia." Jasper sounded like my father when he was angry. His hand moved closer to me.

Henry hung his head as I pulled my wallet from my back pocket and showed Jasper. "It's a picture from when my sisters face painted us."

He took the wallet and looked at the photo in the plastic insert. "Hmm. I can see how this would be embarrassing, Fitch." He called Henry by his last name, something he did when he was mad at someone, and pulled the photo from the plastic sleeve. He proceeded to tear it into a zillion pieces and tucked them into his front pocket. "There ya go, *man*. Gone now." He wiped his hands together. "She has no hold on you now. For blackmail, I mean." Jasper narrowed his eyes.

I almost lost my lunch. I fought back tears when I saw Henry's eyes widen. Embarrassed. I was totally embarrassed Henry witnessed what was soon to be a fight between Jasper and me.

"Oh man, it's cool. I really wasn't worried." The embarrassment in his eyes mirrored mine.

I didn't realize until that moment how much the picture meant to me.

"I'm sorry," Henry mouthed to me as he rode off on his bike.

I waved, but he'd already turned away. "See you at graduation tomorrow," I yelled out to him, despite Jasper's stern look.

3

Graduation Day

I sat between Mack Berg and Pam Bergman at graduation. We were always seated together in our classes alphabetically. Oddly, in a class of 300, we never got to know each other and in fact, rarely spoke. Mack had picked on me since the fourth grade when I threw up in class. Pukey was my nickname for three years, thanks to him, until he threw up his applesauce in the cafeteria during lunch.

Karma. You could always count on it.

He asked me out in tenth grade. I said no, mostly because he'd always teased me. I was saved by a fire drill when the bell rang loudly in my ears. It always made me jump. Rude and unexpected loud alarms. When we returned from the fire drill, Mack asked out the girl in the seat behind me, Jody Brunacini. She'd laughed and said no too. It was not Mack's day.

Today as young adults, we sat properly, hands in our laps and listened to the commencement speaker,

Stuart Landon, the former mayor and now lieutenant governor of our state. As usual my mind wandered. I daydreamed and made mental lists of what I would do after graduation.

My mom and step-dad told me they wouldn't pay for me to go to college. "You'll have to pay for it yourself," Mom had told me while she worked away in her flower bed. "Or get a job, kid." Her voice sounded cold. But, that wasn't anything new. She went on to say they didn't have that kind of money. I had no idea how many bills they paid or how much they were, so I figured they already owed a lot. They had two cars, an RV, and a mortgage. I shrugged and let the subject drop, but not before she told me they made too much money for me to qualify for financial aid since President Reagan made tax and budget cuts to student aid. Mom told me that student assistance and Pell grants had been cut big time. She also complained that subsidized federal loans were now limited to the middle class families, which we were. So, I'd work and hopefully save enough to go in a few years.

I scanned the audience for my mom and step-dad. They sat in the near back of the open air amphitheater, located next to Chautauqua Lake. The warm summer breezes caressed my skin, and cooled the heat my nerves had created. Both my parents stood out. You can't miss a cowboy hat in a sea of naked heads. Phillip, my step-dad, caught my eye and waved. I snuck a little queen wave close to my chest. He grinned at me, and Mom nudged him so he went back to his serious expression. He rarely went anywhere without wearing his cowboy hat and boots. The hat hid his grey bristled buzz cut. He preferred a bolo tie to one made of silk. And he wore half moon glasses around his neck, ready to pop them on when he needed to read something, and he read a lot. I would bet anything he had today's newspaper in his back pocket, folded over to the daily crossword puzzle.

After the 'big walk' everyone emphasizes as being so important, and what my mom called it, the class of 82 tossed their graduation caps in celebration at the end of the ceremony. We walked en masse to the reception hall. Families would be waiting to congratulate their spawn and take photos to show to their friends and co-workers after they got them developed. There would be so many photo orders after graduation, it might take as long as a week to get their photos back from the drug store drop off counter.

That's when it hit me. I didn't have anywhere to go on Monday morning.

I would be free.

I hadn't yet heard back from any of the places I'd applied. There was the bank teller position at First National, which I'd heard had poor benefits, whatever those were. And I'd applied as a counter waitress at Flamingo Bowling Lanes. Also, not promising. There was the cashier position at the Fly Buyz grocery story. And there was the job at the mall in the clothing boutique. I heard they had a great employee discount on clothing.

Now that's a good benefit.

"Hey Emelia, wait up." Henry jogged behind me, empty diploma holder tucked under his arm. We had to return to school on Monday to pick up the actual paper diploma that would go inside. The holder is all we got at graduation. I guess that made it easier than making sure they handed the right diploma to each of the 300 plus graduates.

I stepped off the cobblestone path and walked with Henry as the others hurried and chatted excitedly on their way to the reception hall.

"What's up?" I adjusted my crooked cap and blew the tassel out of my face.

"Nothing." He scratched his chin.

"Oh. Kay." I hooked my elbow with his. "Let's get this party started." I started to walk, but his unmoving stance pulled me back into him. "Oops." I laughed, a little too much. "Henry?" I could see something in his eyes. It reminded me of the look I'd seen on my step-dad's face the day he had to put my mom's dog, Lady, to sleep. "You feeling okay?" I held my hand to his forehead.

He leaned into my hand. "I'm fine." He reached up, took my hand off his forehead, and held it between us. Our gowns concealed them. "Can we just walk slowly? I'm...I'm not in a hurry for this day to end."

"Why? We've talked about this day since ninth grade." He still held my hand. When Jasper's image flashed through my mind, I tugged to pull it free. He held it tight. Something was wrong with my best guy friend. My heart beat a little faster, nervous tingles ran down my spine.

"Yeah. It seemed a lot farther away in ninth grade. I didn't know those four years would disappear with Jimmy Hoffa."

I gave his hand a squeeze. He was nervous like me about starting this new chapter in our lives. "We'll be fine," I assured him.

"Um, Emelia. Um..."

"Listen." I led him away from the others to a bench under an oak tree. A black squirrel scampered away, chattering at us like an angry old woman. I sat and tugged Henry down next to me. "I'm nervous too. I realized about twenty minutes ago I don't *have* to be anywhere tomorrow morning. I ain't gonna lie, I almost had a panic attack. But I realize now I have my magical paper, or at least my empty diploma holder." I waved it at him. "It tells the world I can work. I am capable. I've reached the minimum requirement to move on to the next phase of life. Time to level up like in Donkey Kong. But you, Henry." I sighed. Henry was so smart. And his parents were going to pay for college. "You get to chase your dreams. You're going to Cornell University, my step-dad's alma mater, and you're gonna be great."

He shook his head.

"Yes. You will." I squeezed his hand. Jasper would be big time mad if he saw me sitting alone with Henry, holding his hand. But he wouldn't see me. Jasper had a meeting out of town for the weekend in Atlantic City with his sales company. The benefits of being an adult that I hadn't yet experienced. And he hadn't invited me to go with him either. So lucky me. I could spend some time on this important day, this rite of passage, with my best friend Henry.

Henry looked at me, eyes dark, pupils wide. "No. It's..."

I kept on with my pep talk. "You'll study animal science and come back here to open a veterinary office just in time for Doc Dowd to retire. Remember when we went to his office on a field trip and we talked to him about it? And he also wrote you a letter of recommendation to Cornell. Like my step-dad did for you."

"I know. Look, is it okay if I savor this moment? With you? I'm not really looking forward to being around all those people stuffing their faces with marble cake and punch."

I happened to like marble cake and punch. "Sure. I don't mind. But....cake, Henry?"

He grinned a little bit, which made me smile. His nervousness maybe gone a little bit. "I know how much you love cake."

"Do you feel any better now? About, ya know, all the adult things?"

"I guess so."

I patted his knee and he laid his hand upon mine. My knees knocked together. A shadow caught my eye.

Was that Kelli-Anne on the cobblestone path. I let out a swoosh of air when I looked closer. It turned out to be only the leaves rustling on the trees, casting a moving shadow. "I promise, you'll be fine. You've laid out a good, solid plan. And I'll be your first customer."

"Oh yeah. The crazy cat lady. How many will you be bringing me?"

"Well, I have Muffin already, and I figure I'll get one cat a year. You'll be away for at least six to eight years..."

He held up his hand. "Stop! You can't be serious."

I laid my hand on my heart. "So help me."

He smacked his hand onto his forehead and looked at me and smiled.

I couldn't help but smile right back.

"Thank you, Emelia."

"For? Which time? I'm so amazing, I can't keep track." I arched a brow at him.

"You *are* amazing, Emelia." He rubbed my knuckles, one by one. "I wouldn't have gotten into Cornell without your *amazing* writing skills."

"Ah. You had that college entrance essay down cold. I only gave you a few ideas." I shrugged away the compliment.

"And you helped me write those essays in school, don't forget. I was terrible with grammar and sentence structure before your help." He closed his hand over mine.

I looked at him and smiled.

But he didn't smile. His face was all serious. I looked out at the blooming Dogwoods, glad to be far enough away from them I didn't start to sneeze or get watery eyes. Dogwood was my kryptonite. My one allergy. I still enjoyed their fragrance, from afar, and their beautiful creamy pink flowers.

"Emelia." Henry spoke softly. I was lost in thought about the trees, the hummingbirds fighting at the feeder, and two chickadees whistling in cadence to each other from adjacent trees.

"Yeah?" I loved the sound of the birds. I know. A total geek girl. But birds reminded me of my dad, being ten years old, and things being, or seeming normal to that point. That was one of the few good memories I had of Dad.

"There's something I've been wanting to do all day." Henry broke my reminiscing before I went to the dark place where my dad still lurked.

I turned to him and asked, "What's that?"

He leaned in towards me. "This."

I didn't wait to see what 'this' was, as I had an inkling I knew what 'it' was and I stupidly, without thought, turned my head back to the birds and the trees, and... Henry being my friend. "I have a boyfriend." It came out flat, without emotion. I hadn't intended for my words to sound so cold. He knew I had a boyfriend. Duh, Emelia. He never seemed keen on Jasper, but had always kept his opinions to himself. Well, mostly.

His voice was very near my ear, his breath warm against my cheek. "I hope he knows what a good girl you are." He leaned away as fast as he'd moved in. "A really good girl."

I had no words. I sat in silence and stared ahead. "If he ever thinks, or says different, you have him talk to me. I'll tell him." He pushed his hands against the bench. "I'll tell him what a good girl you are. A great girl. An honest and faithful girl. Yeah, I'll set him straight."

He went on, his words just 'whaa whaas' like the adults on the Peanuts cartoons. I nodded. Agreeing was second nature to me. I was frozen in my seat, afraid to look at my best friend. Afraid to look into his eyes for what I might see there. Where had this all come from? I hadn't seen it coming. We were friends. There was never a clue something like this... feelings like this... would come up. Ever. Was I just a dumb, clueless girl like Jasper always told me? Like my mom had told me? Like my dad had beaten into me?

He stood, held his hand out to me, and helped me to my feet. He lifted my chin to look at him. "If you ever change your mind... if... if things don't work out with you and Jasper, look me up."

We walked in silence to the reception hall. I was still in shock. I didn't know what he was thinking. We hadn't spoken since he tried to kiss me. Why would he kiss me? Or want to kiss me even? I wasn't desirable. I knew I was ugly, dumb, and worthless. I'd been told so all my life, hadn't I? I was lucky Jasper wanted to be with me. Why'd Henry complicate everything? I was numb. This had come out of nowhere. I didn't know how to react or how to go back to being friends with this between us. I was pretty lame. Just the nerd who sang in the church choir. What did I know of relationships, beyond Jasper and me, and what I'd lived through at home?

He walked with me to my family. My sisters giggled when he grabbed their hands and twirled them around one at a time. His 6'4" stature dwarfed my sisters, who were not short by any means. "I'm gonna miss you two." He mussed their hair. He shook hands with Mom and Phillip as they congratulated him. Oh yeah, he was not only going to Cornell, but he was class valedictorian.

Had I congratulated him? I hadn't even told him how great his speech had been.

I choked on the words, cleared the frog in my throat, but still words didn't come.

All smiles from greeting my family, he accepted their congratulations and well wishes. He turned to me and my heart hurt as I watched his smile fade. "Talk to ya later, Emelia." He waved and left to join his family.

And that was the last time I saw Henry Fitch.

4

The Final Straw

When Jasper broke up with me I forgot about Henry. I was a wreck. Jasper took a job promotion within his sales organization an hour away. His manager required that he relocate and he didn't want to turn down the opportunity.

"We had fun. It's not realistic to keep our relationship going at this point." He'd held my hand as I cried quietly in his car.

A shudder of cold ran down my spine. My stomach was a stormy sea that churned back and forth. "I love you, Jasper."

He turned his face towards the driver's side window. "I gotta get going." Jasper's voice was deep, dismissive. "I have to start my new job tomorrow." He opened the door behind me and I almost toppled onto the pavement in front of my house.

"So, that's it?" I looked into the car, hands on my hips, and waited for Jasper to say something. Something that started with *we can make this work*.

"Don't get all dramatic." He started his car and looked at me without a hint of emotion. "I understand your loss. I'm the best you've had, or ever will have. Don't forget that." He pulled the door shut and drove away.

What did that mean? I wondered, my stomach was nauseous. I went behind Mom's rose bushes and threw up.

I met Tom a couple weeks later. He went through my line at Fly Buyz several times before he asked me out to a movie. He was nice, a law student from Buff State. We had a good enough time at the movie for him to ask me out dancing the following weekend. He was really nice, but he wasn't Jasper. I was lonely with Jasper and Henry both gone now. I needed to do something besides work and sit in my room every night, so I made the attempt of going out with someone else.

Jasper called me out of the blue one day and invited me to dinner with his boss and boss's girlfriend. He also said he wanted to talk to me about us. So we went on a double date. I was a little nervous after not seeing him for almost a month. And a little thrilled that he wanted to try and work things out with me. It ended up being a nice dinner, for the most part. We chatted, laughed, and all got along great. Then it got weird. When Jasper and his boss went outside for a smoke, the girlfriend looked at me like she'd just failed a final exam. Out of the blue she said, "I hope we can be friends. You're a real nice person and I hope you're not mad at me."

Why would I be mad at someone I'd never met? I shrugged and said, "Sure."

After dinner, I followed Jasper in my car to his apartment. He wanted to give me the tour of his place and talk for a bit. Jasper banged his shin on his coffee table, knocking his ashtray onto the floor. I bent to clean it up and noticed more than one brand of cigarettes. Butts that were not Jasper's were mingled with his filterless cigarettes. I remembered the long, slender filter as the same brand that Jasper's boss's girlfriend had.

"How long has Gabe been dating Sophia?" I wiped ashes from my jeans' pant leg.

"Not long. A month or so."

"What are her cigarette butts doing in your ashtray?" I threw up a little bile and choked it back down. What had Jasper done during our month long break up?

"Look." He wiped his brow. "You're imagining things. Those are mine."

"You hate menthol."

"You're just trying to start a fight."

"They *are* hers, aren't they?" He said nothing. "Now I understand why she asked me if I was mad at her. She knew you were dating me when you got

25

together." I remembered something else from dinner. "And you seemed to be consoling her tonight as well."

"What are you talking about?" He placed a finger against his lips.

"I saw you and her talking by the end of the bar when you went to get drinks. You were holding hands and her head was down. She looked... sad. I thought you were consoling her about a fight she maybe had with Gabe. But it was about you."

"What? You're crazy. You heard her wrong. And you're seeing things." He rubbed his eyes. "I was handing her a drink. We weren't holding hands."

Had I heard and seen wrong? I shook my head, confused. I didn't think I had. "You needed me there tonight so your boss didn't know you'd been with his girlfriend."

He turned his back to me and walked to the kitchen.

I didn't need this crap. I gathered my purse, slipped on my flats, and headed to the door. This was it. I had to move on. "Good-bye, Jasper." It hurt my heart to say those words, but I needed to make a clean break. There was no discussing us or fixing this. It had been over since the first time he ended it with me.

He never turned around. "Bye. Don't let the door hit you on the ass on your way out."

What. The. Hell? I opened the front door slowly, half-thinking he'd take me in his arms, apologize, and tell me it was all a misunderstanding. That's what guys did in the movies.

But there were no footsteps behind me and this wasn't a movie.

It was after midnight when I got home. I'd driven back listening to my *Eagles* cassette, crying the entire way. Stupid *New Kid in Town* made me cry all the harder. It was really over between Jasper and me.

And I'd blown off a nice law student for this heartache? I had been honest with Tom when I accepted a date with Jasper. I'd been hopeful we'd get back together and didn't want to lead Tom on.

I walked into the house as quiet as I could, careful not to rattle the key in the door knob. My step-dad was in the kitchen eating ice cream and maple cream cookies. Mom had him on a strict diet. Since retiring a year ago, he'd gained a lot of weight, but he still loved his maple walnut ice cream and cookies.

He eyed me, spoon held at his lips with a heaping helping of ice cream. "I won't tell Mom if you don't."

I gave him a thumbs up and tried to scurry to my room before the tears fell. I needed to be alone to cry, a real snotty nosed cry. I couldn't do it while driving and expect to stay on the road. There were deer, opossum, and raccoons crossing the road at night that I needed to avoid. And the occasional cow that had escaped from a pasture.

"What's up, Emelia Bedelia?" Phillip called to me before I could make my escape. He often called me the name from the beloved children's book. Only her name was spelled Amelia. Mine was spelled like my great-grandma who moved to the United States from Sweden in the late 1800s.

His kindness broke me. I sat in the chair next to him, but as much as I tried to get the words out, there was no sound.

"It's okay." He pulled me to his barrel chest. "Being young is tough." I heard him set his spoon in his dish. He wrapped his other arm around me as well and hugged me tight, while I cried on his shoulder. "It's corny to say this, but true; time heals all wounds. This will pass, 'Melia. It doesn't feel like it now, but it will."

He handed me a napkin from the table. I dried my eyes, my cheeks, and blew my nose. "Thanks, Phillip."

"We love you." His hazel eyes looked sad. I'd put that sad look there.

"Love you too." I stood up. "I'm tired. Gonna go to bed now."

"Emelia."

"Yeah?" I stopped at the foot of the stairs.

"He doesn't deserve you." His eyes looked misty.

I nodded and ran up the stairs. His heart was in the right place, but those words didn't ring true because I didn't deserve Jasper. He'd told me himself he was the best I'd ever have. I wasn't good enough for anyone else.

I made it to the bathroom in time to throw up.

5

Missing Him

I awoke with crusty eyelids and a gravelly gut. I needed food. But, I needed a shower more.

A banging on the bathroom door shortened my relaxing, shower. "Hurry up! I have to get ready for school."

Alexis. I forgot it was Monday. The girls had school.

"Sorry, I'm getting out now." I turned off the hot, soul-soothing liquid. After tying my robe around my waist, I opened the door and stepped aside for Alexis.

"About time" she snarked, pushing past me and slamming the door behind her.

Nice. Just what I needed. "Good morning to you too, Alexis." I spoke through the closed door.

"Rough morning, Emelia?" Andrea, my youngest and more charming sister, was dressed and ready for school. The achiever and make-Mom-proud sister. I loved her to pieces. She had a heart as big as Texas and was the least annoying sister. Most likely why she was Mom's obvious favorite child.

"That would sum it up." I threw my arms in the air.

Out of nowhere she hugged me. "Don't take this wrong, but you look like crap."

I laughed. She was always candid and sometimes honest to a fault.

"I suppose I do." A sob tried to escape my throat, but I choked it down. Three hours of sleep always made me look and feel like crap.

"Ugh, Jasper?" Andrea tilted her head and waited for my response.

Tears forced their way out of my eyes. I blinked and blinked again, but it was too late.

"What's wrong, 'Melia?" She put a hand on my shoulder.

"Jasper and I are done. For good this time." The words seemed to drain me and I slumped to the floor. I wrapped my arms around my knees and pulled into myself. I had just started to get over Jasper, even date someone new, when he'd pulled me back in. He'd given me hope only to crush me all over again.

"I'm sorry." Andrea stood and looked at me, maybe not sure what she should do. "Want me to get Mom?"

"No!"

She drew back.

"Sorry. I didn't mean to yell. I'll be all right. I want to be alone and work through it."

She sat next to me, splaying her pleated skirt around her. "I wish I could make you feel better." Andrea rubbed my shoulder. "I'm just not good at it."

She was so much better at it than she knew. I smiled at her. Twelve, smart, and not a clue how to be social. She was serious and focused on academics. While in contrast, Alexis was on the phone all the time to boys, or to girls talking about the boys.

"You're making me feel better just being you."

"I don't understand how it helps, but I'm glad it does."

We sat in silence. Only the sound of water running in Alexis' shower and the squeak of the hamster wheel, belonging to Andrea, dared break the somber silence.

"I miss Henry." Andrea broke the hush comfortably resting between us. "He always knew how to make you feel better."

"How did he do that?" I hadn't thought of Henry until Andrea mentioned him. How was he doing at college?

She rubbed her chin. "Like the time you got dressed in your pretty pink ruffled top and new jeans to go to a movie with Jasper. You waited on the porch for hours and he didn't show."

"Hmm. I remember that night. He didn't answer his phone, either." I rubbed the throbbing at my temples.

"Henry peddled by with his football tucked under his arm, going to meet some friends at the park. He saw you on the porch and stopped to talk to you. You two were laughing and having so much fun, he forgot about the park. And you forgot about Jasper not showing up."

"Hmm," I smiled at the thought of the memory.

"Henry cheered me up too. He's good at making people laugh. Remember when I was going to a Girl Scout meeting and I fell in the mud in my new uniform?"

"Oh yeah." My heart dropped. Mom had been so mad at Andrea for ruining her new uniform. It had been the only time I'd seen Mom mad at her.

"Henry was walking by on his way to basketball practice. He pulled me out of the mud and gave me some gum he had in his backpack. And not just one piece, either. The entire pack!"

I laughed. "Henry was never without gum."

"And he bought ten boxes of cookies from me when I was selling them. It was my best order ever. He was my best Girl Scout cookie customer."

"He really was. You know, he always gave me two boxes of the cheddar crackers. He told me he didn't want to be the only one getting fat off your cookies."

We laughed at the memory and talking about Henry made me feel better.

"And 'Melia, don't forget when Jasper had to go out of town during homecoming week."

I remembered. I'd already bought a new dress and shoes. Jasper had promised to take me, and at the last minute he had to go out of town for sales management training for his job.

"Emelia, Henry turned your frown around when he took you to the dance. Even though he was going to stay home and watch a movie for a paper he had due on Monday."

I smiled. "Oh yeah. Henry was the best friend a girl could ever have."

"You came home from the dance twirling around the living room and singing a song you love. Oh, what was it?" She snapped her fingers.

"*Dancing in the Moonlight*. Yeah, it was the last dance at homecoming. That turned out to be a great night." I could still see how handsome he'd been in his black dress pants and blue tie.

"See? Henry always knew how to cheer you up. And me too. If he were here now, he'd have you smiling in no time." Her eyes looked a little dreamy. Did she have a little crush on Henry?

"Sis, can't you see the smile on my face now?" I tickled her belly and she laughed. "You put this smile here."

"Yeah, I guess I did."

"Thanks Andrea."

She smiled. "Where is Henry? He doesn't visit anymore."

"He went to college, remember?"

"Duh." She scowled at me. "But I guess I thought he'd come and visit us when he visits his parents."

"Oh, his parents moved to Arizona. Or Colorado. Or maybe Nevada? I don't know. Henry never told me." I shrugged.

Andrea let out a big sigh. "Emelia, why wasn't Henry your boyfriend instead of Jasper? Jasper never made you laugh or smile like Henry did. And he wasn't very nice to me." She crossed her arms.

My heart clutched. "Henry was my best guy friend. Not my boyfriend." The memory from graduation flooded back. The way he'd held my hand and looked at me; nobody had ever looked at me with such intensity. How could I have known how he felt? How could I have betrayed Jasper at that point? We'd been friends for so long, and I hadn't thought of him as anything more.

"Phillip says Mom is his best friend. They love each other. Why couldn't you and Henry love each other?"

"We did. As friends. But just friends."

Andrea grabbed both sides of her head. "All this relationship stuff is so confusing."

"It is, you're right. So don't rush into any relationships." I wagged my finger at her.

"Don't worry, I won't. Who needs it?" She stood, adjusted her skirt, and pulled up her knee socks. "I have to go." She waved. I blew her a kiss, which she caught and tucked into her pocket.

She never missed a kiss. I guess it was our thing.

Andrea never missed anything else either. She got me thinking about Henry and why I hadn't heard from him.

Abruptly, the bathroom door swung open and Alexis emerged. Hands akimbo, she scowled down at me. "Why are you still here?"

I couldn't resist to say, "Peeking through the keyhole."

She pursed her lips, "You're weird. There is no keyhole."

"Hmm," I let her wonder what I was doing. Unlike Andrea, Alexis was a fifteen-year old mini Mom: distant, cold, and aloof.

While she stomped off to her room and slammed the door, my mind went to Henry and his whereabouts.

Time to play detective.

6

One Red Heart

It wasn't that I never tried to find Henry. I'd called information for Henry's number so I could wish him a happy birthday in October. There was no number listed. Social media sites weren't a thing in 1982. Cell phones didn't exist either. I'd heard from customers at Fly Buyz that Henry's family moved after graduation. They'd sold their home and moved to parts unknown, and left no forwarding address. I'd heard a rumor they'd moved west for the drier climate. Henry's mom had arthritis. Some of the gossip around town was they'd owed a lot of money and left town. Others gossiped they'd gone bankrupt paying for Henry's college education. Some figured they'd sold their home to pay for it. Henry was the Fitches only child. A late-in-life baby my mom called him. I didn't know his parents. Henry had never invited me to his house. We only hung out at school or on my porch mostly. He'd never mentioned any other family and I never thought to ask.

I started my search for Henry the next day, after I caught up on some much-needed sleep. I'd slept the rest of the morning and all afternoon. The mirror revealed swollen, red eyes when I awoke. The smell of something good cooking wafted up the stairs.

I covered my swollen eyes the best I could with concealer and powder, then doused my eyes with Visine. I headed downstairs to see what was cooking. Mom and Phillip were at the small kitchenette set with bowls in front of them. I inhaled, "Mmm, smells good."

"Mom's chili." Phillip wiped his mouth with his napkin.

I went to the crockpot and looked for a serving or two. When had I last eaten?

"There isn't any left." Mom never looked at me, she rarely did. I looked like Dad, I was a reminder of their failed marriage. Their loveless marriage. The failed attempt to save a marriage by having kids. How many times had she told me she'd decided to have my sisters and me to save her marriage to Dad? Enough to burn the words into my mind permanently. It's sad when you realize your fate was determined before you exited the womb. Created to save a loveless marriage and doomed to a loveless childhood. No matter what I did, I didn't stand a chance. I would never be good enough. Never measure up. And never be loved. She was indifferent to my presence. We were little unwanted critters stored in the attic bedrooms, like in that book everyone was reading. Maybe if she hadn't been pressured by her church to fix the marriage, as though it only takes one to save a marriage, she would have gotten a divorce sooner and had a happier life. And not been stuck with three failed attempts to make her life better. I couldn't be mad at her, she'd tried her best. I remembered the time at church when people whispered about her and stared at her. Her counseling sessions with her pastor hadn't been confidential as she had thought they would be. I remember her crying all the way home. I wasn't very old but I knew about bullies from school. And I knew my mom had been bullied.

I reminded her of Dad and all his failings, and their failed marriage.

I groaned, put the lid back on the pot, and opened the fridge. Nothing. Some skim milk, jalapeño cheese, and peach yogurt.

"If you got up earlier, maybe you would have gotten some." Mom's spoon scraped the bottom of her bowl.

Right. It didn't matter when I got up. Meals were always made for two. Sometimes Andrea got some. Alexis rarely ate unless it was chocolate or Pepsi. She smoked and I didn't know how she could afford the 85 cents per pack. I didn't want to know. I'd smelled bacon cooking many Sunday mornings and jumped out of bed hoping to get some. It was my favorite. But there was always only enough for two.

I shut the fridge and grabbed my coat. "Where's Andrea and Alexis?"

"They haven't come home from school yet. Where are you going now?" Mom looked at me through narrowed eyelids.

"To get something to eat."

Mom stood and went to the door. "You are not going out again." She held her arms across the door and glared at me.

"Mom, I need to get something to eat."

"We have food here."

I shook my head and went to the front door. I should have grabbed something at Fly Buyz when I got paid last week.

"Phillip, don't let her out the front door."

Phillip went to the door and stretched out his arms in front of it, his face expressionless.

"C'mon, Phillip." I tried to duck under his arms.

He shook his head but didn't say a word. He had to do what Mom requested of him if he wanted peace.

My blood boiled. I'd had enough for two days. I didn't want to argue. I grabbed some saltines from the kitchen table and a glass of water and headed back to my room.

"Where are you going? Get back down here." Mom's voice rasped from the bottom of the stairs.

"Why?"

"You can help out around here. Like do the dishes." She pointed to the sink.

"Okay." I shrugged, set the crackers and glass on the steps, and went to the sink. Filling the sink with water, I rolled up my sleeves. I fought the tears threatening to spill out onto my cheeks. I wanted to be left alone. My stomach twisted into itself. It rebelled because I hadn't fed it for who knew how long.

The kitchen door flung open and the wind blew in Alexis and Andrea. Andrea gave me a hug around the neck. She whispered so only I could hear. "Feel any better?"

I shrugged. "I will be better when I can eat."

"I have some corn chips and a soda from the school store. I'll leave it in the usual hiding place."

"Thank you." She often brought home treats from the school store where she volunteered. She'd buy expired chips and snacks half off with her lunch money and share with me.

Alexis grabbed the peach yogurt from the fridge and went upstairs. I followed soon after when I'd finished the dishes, dried them, and put them away.

I locked my bedroom door and retrieved the corn chips and soda from my clogs in the back of my closet. Alexis was prone to scout and pillage my room. Nothing was off limits to her. She'd never bothered with my clogs yet. My feet were two sizes bigger than hers, so my shoes were safe. I was grateful because the chips tasted heavenly, and the soda chaser was the perfect pairing. I kept my best tops, clogs, and Candies hidden in the back of my closet under a ripped sheet. Only Andrea knew about them. My clothes didn't fit her anyway.

A note slid under my door. I got off the bed to retrieve it. Upon opening it, I smiled. A red heart, colored in with red crayon, had been drawn in the middle of the lined notebook paper. Under it, in Andrea's hand writing, were the words *God loves you and so do I.*

Her kind words took me to Sob Town once again. I cried myself to sleep and didn't wake until morning.

The day I tried to find Henry.

7

The Lie

I called directory assistance and got the number to Cornell University admissions. Henry had mentioned he would be living on campus and I'd hoped to get an address or a phone number to his dorm. It was early January 1983. Information wasn't available at our fingertips. People weren't so concerned with privacy either.

I wasn't so fortunate.

"What was your name again?" The raspy voiced woman at the other end asked. I heard her exhale in a rapid swoosh before she let out a phlegmy-sounding cough. I waited for her to catch her breath before I responded to her question.

"Emelia Berggren. I'm looking for a phone number for Henry Fitch. He started school in the fall. I believe he moved in at the beginning of summer."

"Young lady, I can't give out that information." She exhaled a big breath, and the nasty cough again.

"Can you connect me to his room?"

She was quiet and I heard her rustling through papers.

"Or an address. I can write him a letter. It doesn't matter, I'll drive out there if I have to and see him in person."

"I wouldn't waste your time, sweetie."

Was that a little bit of compassion? "He's my best friend. It wouldn't be a waste of time."

"If he's your best friend, shouldn't you *have* his contact information already? Wouldn't he have given it to you?" Her voice oozed with accusation.

I wiped the sweat from my brow. "It's complicated. We went our own ways after graduation. I want to connect with him again."

"I guess it doesn't matter if I tell you this." She let out a long breath and coughed again. "He doesn't attend Cornell."

"What do you mean he doesn't go to Cornell?" My heart pounded against my ribs.

"He isn't registered for any classes. He's not a student. Sorry. You must have the wrong information."

"No. I'm sure of it. We talked about it for two years. Him going to Cornell. My step-dad gave him a letter of reference."

"What's your step-dad's name?"

"Phillip. Phillip Armstrong."

Again rustling papers. "Let me check something. I'm going to put you on hold."

"Okay." But she was already gone. I drummed the pencil by the phone against the kitchen counter, keeping beat with the 50s Doo Wop music on hold. From my seat on the stool next to the wall phone, I checked the clock over the stove to see if anyone was expected home soon. It was a little after ten. The girls were in school and Mom was working. I didn't know what errand Mom had sent Phillip on, but he could be back at any minute.

While I waited on hold, I noticed a book on the counter in front of me. It was open and parts of it were highlighted. I lifted the cover to read the title, *Psychology for Supervisors*. It must have been one of Phillip's college textbooks. He'd been an engineer before he retired. He'd also been the supervisor for his department, which made sense as to why he had the book. But why was he reading it now that he was retired? Maybe he was going to go back to work. I read what he had highlighted under *Detrimental Personality Disorders in the Work Environment*.

Narcissistic Personality Disorder

Narcissism is a chronic disorder that affects the person for several years or for life. It is incurable. The main reason - the person with Narcissistic Personality Disorder doesn't assume any responsibility for their actions. The disorder is most common in men. The cause is not known.

Symptoms of narcissistic personality disorder include:

An exaggerated sense of self-importance, preoccupation with fantasies of success, power, money, intelligence, good looks, or perfect love. They believe they are special and only other special people appreciate their greatness. They are irresponsible with money. They have a disproportionate need for admiration. They have a false sense of entitlement. They lie and distort the facts. They are emotionally distant. They are very controlling. They exploit others for their own gain without any guilt....

That sounded a little like Jasper, didn't it? He talked about being successful all the time, and having lots of money someday. He prided himself on being well-groomed, well-dressed, and made sure to get a haircut every four weeks like clockwork. I laughed at my own thoughts. Jasper worked hard and earned his promotions. He had to look nice for his job. He didn't have this narcissistic disorder thing. Although, he had worked hard to get Vance out of the manager position in their office and had stepped into Vance's position seamlessly. That hadn't lasted long before he'd moved into Dawson's position as the district sales manager over the tri-state area. What had he told me? Something about Dawson not responding to his phone calls and giving his accounts to the other sales reps. He called his corporate manager almost nightly to fill him in on Dawson's failings. *Emelia, there you go overthinking again,* I could almost hear Jasper saying. Yet, I couldn't ignore the fact he had moved into his new management position in Erie rather soon. I read a little further down the highlighted section.

Signs you may be dealing with a narcissist:

They gaslight you. The signs of this include: no longer feeling like the person you once were, feeling anxious and having low self-esteem, you feel like you're being overly sensitive, you feel you can't do anything right....

I questioned myself all the time, but that's because I *couldn't* do anything right. I made Jasper mad a lot and that is why I had to question everything I said and did before I did it, so Jasper wouldn't get mad at me. I looked at the words again, *feeling anxious and having low self-esteem.* How often had Jasper told me I didn't have any self-esteem? And I didn't. But that's because I wasn't good at anything. I messed up whatever I tried. I was anxious all the time and nervous about everything. I could never pinpoint the cause of the anxiety but guessed it had something to do with school or my hormones. That always made my stomach ache, too.

"Emelia?" The woman's raspy voice was back on the line. I pushed away the textbook and shook myself out of my thoughts. "I found the file for your step-dad. He was a student here back in the 50s. And there is a copy of the letter he wrote on Mr. Fitch's behalf. But the file for Mr. Fitch has only a few papers in it: your step-dad's letter, one from a Mr. Dowd, his application, and acceptance letter. Your information is correct. It's just there is no Henry. He's not here."

I lowered my head into my hand. Had Henry lied about where he was going? That was out of character for him. He'd discussed his plans to go to Cornell on more than a few occasions. He would live on campus. He would go in early summer to work and make some money to pay for school expenses. He didn't want to put the entire burden on his aging parents.

"Are you still there, Ms. Berggren?"

"Yes."

"I'm sorry I can't help you. I can't give you the information you need. Good luck finding your friend."

"Thank you."

I hung up the receiver as Phillip walked through the door with two bags of groceries.

He unpacked them onto the table: cat food, yogurt, bananas, milk, orange juice, and a loaf of bread. The essentials around here.

He didn't say anything, just cleared his throat while he put away the groceries. Things were still awkward between us since yesterday's confrontation. I decided it was my cue to slip out and up to my room.

I'd struck out looking for Henry. He wasn't where he told me he'd be. Or had I heard wrong? That would be like me to screw it up.

Maybe he wasn't at Cornell, but he might be at another area school. I pulled out my Atlas from my desk drawer. It had been a travel companion on the road to Wyoming with a group of Girl Scouts the summer before high school in '79. The 1700-mile trip took three weeks.

We'd made stops at significant landmarks along the way like: Devil's Tower, Mount Rushmore, the Grand Canyon. We'd stayed at state parks, which was a drag because there wasn't anything there to do. And the last night, we'd stopped at a KOA and drooled over the pool and all the other teens.... boys.... a game room. Civilization at last after almost three long weeks of roughing it in tents. But the girl in charge of lodging, Jennifer, concurred with the two adult chaperones that it was too expensive and we should go to a state park. Seriously? No lie. We'd scrimped and saved all the money we'd fundraised before the trip. It had taken two years of garage sales and cookie sales to raise enough money for the adventure. We'd gone cheap the entire trip. We wanted this one last hurrah of fun. But, we'd wound up at a state park in the boondocks of West Virginia. We built a campfire, made some kind of foil dinner, and sang camp songs in the dark, while I dreamed of swimming in a heated pool and talking to the cute guys who did cannonballs and laughed. I was certain they were having more fun than we were.

Jennifer was not popular that night. I'd heard someone put a fat, juicy toad in her tent. I have no idea who would have done such a horrible thing to her.

I laughed, flipping the pages of my Atlas to New York State. I located Cornell in Ithaca. Maybe I'd misunderstood and he'd gone to Ithaca college. It was probably a little less expensive than an Ivy League school like Cornell. There was a state university in

Cortland. And also Elmira. And Syracuse, Binghamton, and Corning Community College were options as well. At least I'd heard Phillip talk about his days at Cornell enough I recognized the names of the nearby towns. And he'd talked about Ithaca College. I suppose I could ask Phillip. But, he'd want to know why and I didn't want to get into it with him. I wasn't ready to talk with him yet.

Maybe Henry had changed his mind and I didn't know about it. Or I hadn't listened well enough to retain that important nugget of information. I'd always been prattling on about Jasper. Had I been an inconsiderate friend? I certainly hadn't been a very good one to wait so long to look for Henry.

My heart hurt. I hadn't realized I missed Henry until now. I really was an awful friend.

The image of his face after I'd turned from his attempted kiss entered my mind and my heart hurt worse. I shook it off. I had things to do after all. I got my notebook and a pen and jotted down a list of possible Henry locations: Ithaca, Cortland, Elmira, Binghamton, Syracuse, and Corning. It was a good start. I'd call directory assistance for listings of a Henry Fitch in those areas first. If nothing panned out, I could try the smaller neighboring towns. He may be living off campus in a more rural area. He always liked the country: swimming holes, dirt bikes, and climbing trees.

I doodled on the paper, waiting for the sound of the door to close when Phillip left to meet my mom for lunch. They dined every day together at McDonalds, so an adoring Phillip could spend time with Mom, and Mom didn't have to spend her half hour lunch break running home, making a lunch, and getting back to work. Half hour lunch breaks suck. Phillip would leave ten minutes early and order her meal and have it waiting for her.

He really did love my mom. I suppose it's easy to love someone when they treat you like you're the only other person in the world.

I would eat liver for a week for that kind of love.

8

Hope

At the sound of the station wagon crunching on our gravel driveway, I grabbed my list and went to the kitchen to use the phone. First, I made a peanut butter sandwich and poured a glass of milk. My fingers turned the rotary dial on the wall phone: 5-5-5-1-2-1-2.

"City and State, please." The woman's voice crackled through the bad connection on the phone line.

"Ithaca, New York."

"Name?"

"Fitch. Henry Fitch."

"One moment, please."

She did whatever she does: look through a massive phone book perhaps, maybe one for each county and state, or maybe she had a computer where she looked him up. It would be handy to have my own computer, as if. I didn't make enough money in a year to pay for one. My parents certainly couldn't afford one.

"I have no listing for a Henry Fitch in Ithaca." The operator was back on the line. "Would you like me to try another city?"

"Yes, please." I crossed Ithaca off my list and named off the next one. "Syracuse."

"Same name?"

"Yes."

"One moment please." The sound of her fingernails clicking on a keyboard answered my question as to how she looked up her information.

"Sorry. No Henry Fitch in Syracuse either. Would you like me to try the surrounding areas?"

"Yes, please. And could you check Elmira and Binghamton too?"

"Yes ma'am." More clicking.

My heart couldn't take it. Henry couldn't have just vanished, could he?

"I'm sorry. I've tried all the surrounding areas and there is no Henry Fitch. Is there anything else I can do for you?"

Sure. Move on to the next caller as if my breath didn't hang on this very moment. "No. Thank you anyways."

And with a click, she was gone.

What now? Just let Henry go without ever thinking of him again? There was a little catch in my throat, something I couldn't push down.

I needed air. I grabbed my windbreaker and booked it. Staring at the cracks in the sidewalk, I headed towards town. The air was crisp. January could be a mishmash of a thaw, which brought warm temperatures and sunshine, or subzero cold temperatures, with wind and power outages. Today was the somewhere in-between

The game room was open. My old hang from high school. Why not? Maybe some jukebox music and a game of space invaders would chill me out.

"Hey Rosalina." The kind-hearted proprietor and co-owner of Uncle Pips wiped down the counter when I came in.

"Emelia. It's been a long time. How have you been?" She came over and gave me a big hug. She was like a second mother to everyone who hung out here.

"I'm good, Rosa. How have you been? Johnny behaving?" Johnny, her husband, worked nights and Rosa worked the day shift.

"Eh, men, you know?" She elbowed me and smiled.

Yeah, I knew all too well.

"What have you been doing since graduation?" She wiped off a red padded stool at the counter and motioned for me to sit.

"Working at the Fly Buyz. Day off today."

"Hmm. And you wandered in here. Why today, Emelia? Something got you down?"

"What?"

Rosalina knows the look. "It's a guy, isn't it?"

Two guys. "Oh, it's just...I'm trying to find Henry."

"Is he lost?" She rang up a pop and chips for a red-haired little dweeb who should have been in school at this time of day.

"To me he is. He went off to Cornell at the end of last summer and I haven't heard from him. Not since graduation day." Not since I'd acted like a jerk.

"I'm sorry I can't help you. I haven't seen him since the day before graduation."

That was the day he'd been at my house, until Jasper chased him away. "Did he say anything about where he was going to school?"

"Hmmm, I don't recall. He brought me a box of chocolates and a card from the corner drugstore. He thanked me for all the hours Johnny and me put up with him and his late night studying."

"Studying?" That was news to me.

"Sure sweetie. He'd come here at night and on Saturdays when he needed a place to concentrate."

"How could he concentrate here? With all the music and the noise of the foosball table. Omigod, and the yelling when they fight over a shot. How did Henry concentrate with all the noise?"

"It was better than the noise at home, sweetie. You must know?"

"No. Henry never mentioned home. Or his parents. He told me he was an only child and his parents were old." Henry hadn't mentioned much about his home or family. Why hadn't I ever asked?

"Doesn't surprise me. But I've said too much. And Henry never liked the spotlight on himself." Rosa pulled a fresh, hot pizza sub from the ancient black pizza oven and handed it to a dropout-burnout standing at the end of the counter.

"I guess not. In the four years I'd known him, we only talked about essays and writing and college. And Jasper."

"Your boyfriend Jasper?"

"Ex-boyfriend." I corrected her.

"Mmm hmm. I see." Rosa sprinkled mozzarella cheese on a sauce covered sub roll before placing the pizza paddle in the hot oven and slamming the heavy door closed with her shoulder. "Jasper wasn't right for you. Too old, too... grown. A young girl needs a nice young man who can share in the growings of life together. But enough of that business. What would Henry say about Jasper?"

"Not much. When Jasper and I fought, Henry tried to cheer me up. He'd say it would be okay and we'd go get ice cream at the Tasty Shack. Or we'd walk to HoJo's and get french fries and Cokes. And he was always right, because Jasper would come back to me." I took a sip of the pop Rosa slid in front of me. The fizzing soda reminded me of the time Henry and I walked to HoJo's after the last big fight I had with Jasper. Henry bought me a soda and it had taken a couple refills before talking to him made me feel better. I also remembered Henry had told me I'd given Jasper too many chances. He'd said I shouldn't take him back again. That was the first time he'd ever said that. He'd even called Jasper a huge jerk for treating me the way he had. I didn't want to tell Rosa about that though. "But not this time. We are really through."

"He must have done something bad this time." Rosa sat on the stool behind the counter, and wiped her forehead with her apron. Sitting in front of a pizza oven was warm and cozy on a wet winter day. To Rosa, the heat must have felt more like an August afternoon.

"He did. And... I wanted to talk to Henry about it. He always makes things better."

"Sweetie, isn't that a little selfish?"

I choked on my Coke. "How is it selfish?" Although I'd asked the question, I knew the answer. What did I really know about Henry? What had I really asked him about his life?

"Henry obviously had a crush on you."

"I..." I couldn't deny it now. Not since he'd tried to kiss me at graduation. Looking back, I could see it. But at the time, I had no clue. "I didn't know. He was always so fun and friendly. I figured we were just that. Friends. But," I twirled the ends of my hair. "He never told me how he felt until graduation day."

Rosa smiled wide. "Ah, I wondered if he would."

"You knew?"

"Yes. He spent a lot of time here. We talked sometimes. Mostly, he studied or banged around on the foosball table. But one night, a slow night, we had a nice talk, Henry and I. He beat around the bush a lot, but I got the gist of what he was saying. He thought you were the, what's it kids say these days, the bomb?"

I laughed. "Rosa, seriously."

She wasn't laughing. "The way he looked at you when you were talking to your friends or playing the space invaders machine, darling, I would love it if Johnny ever looked at me the way Henry looked at you. Lord knows, he might have back before I had my three babies, but now, no. No, I can't say as I've ever seen any man look at a gal the way he looked at you." Rosa pulled open the pizza oven to check on her sub. "And most telling was the way he looked at Jasper those couple times he came in here with you. Daggers. And he'd look at you with the saddest eyes." Rosa rubbed at her cheek. "I don't interfere, mind you, nope. I mind my own business. But sweetie, that sweet boy had it for you bad. And I sure don't think he wants to be the fall guy now."

My skin prickled. "What do you mean by that?"

"Don't run to him because Jasper and you are done. Don't use him that way. If you run to him, you do it because you want to be with him the way I suspect he wants to be with you."

"Not anymore. I'm pretty sure I broke his heart. I didn't mean to. I didn't know." I hung my head and stared into my reflection on top of the Coke can. "I just didn't know. And if I could go back to that day..."

"Yes dear. We all have regrets. Can't change it. Just have to move forward and do the best we can."

But I could change it. I could go back.

I put a dollar on the counter and headed towards the door. "Gotta run, Rosa. Thank you!"

"What'd I do?"

"You gave me hope."

9

Crossroads

I ran past Phillip and upstairs to my room. I tossed my room trying to find it. It wasn't in my jewelry box. I know I'd put it there. I upended my laundry basket and searched the pockets of all my pants and jeans. Nothing. At my desk, I scattered my papers in hopes I'd taken it off and set it there, too tired to put in where it belonged. Not. There. "This sucks!" I stepped over the papers to my bed and pulled out what was underneath, a shoebox and a cigar box my mom had given me from the drug store where she worked. I rifled through the contents of both and came up empty. Muffin, my cat, looked at me with a sleepy gaze from the foot of my bed. After a wide yawn, she tucked her head back under her paw and continued with her cat nap.

"What are you doing?" Alexis stood in my doorway, unlit cigarette in hand.

"Looking for something. Don't you think you should put that thing away?" I pointed at her cigarette.

"Phillip catches you with that, you're never gonna hear the end of it."

She shrugged her shoulders. "I'm going for a walk when he leaves to pick up Mom. He won't know." She flicked her Bic near my face. "And what are you looking for?"

"Why aren't you in school?"

She put the back of her hand on her forehead. "Sick. Had to stay home."

"Bogus."

"I don't give a crap what you think." She raised her voice. "So, you still haven't answered my question." She crossed her arms and tapped her foot.

"What question?"

"What. Are. You. Doing?" She emphasized each word louder than the one before it.

"I'm trying to find something."

"That's obvious. What kind of something?"

"It's a necklace."

"What's it look like?"

Alexis was way too curious about what I was doing, which led me to believe she was hiding something. I sat back on my haunches, looked at her, and held out my hand. "Give it back to me, Alexis."

"What? I don't have anything." She took a step backwards.

She liked to pilfer items from my room when I wasn't home. Usually, she took clothing or little trinkets that really didn't matter much to me. But this mattered. I scrambled to my feet and lunged at her before she could run into her room and lock the door.

"Get off me!" She squirmed from my grasp, but I still had a hold of her pink bath robe. "Give me that." She held out her hand.

"I wonder what we have in our pockets today." I smiled at her with maliciousness pouring from my soul for what she took from me. I also knew she held her most treasured items in her robe's huge, fluffy pockets. She lived in this robe when she wasn't at school or the mall. She and her best friend Fern were total mall rats.

She grabbed at me, but I pulled the robe behind my back. I searched the pockets and felt her pack of cigarettes, her lighter, a few wads of paper, and something metal.

"You're a major bitch!" She fumbled behind me, trying to retrieve her shroud.

"Here you go." I tossed it over her head. "Stay out of my shit, or I'll let Mom and Phillip in on your pocket stash."

She yanked the robe from her head and scrunched her mouth into an 'O'. She stomped to her room while properly giving me the finger before she slammed the door.

I held up the necklace and smiled. "Let's see what happens with this thing."

I locked my bedroom door and sat cross-legged on my green and pink shag carpet. The time twister dangled from my fingertips, twirling in the sunlight, beckoning me to give it a go. I pulled it in close to read the small words etched on the edge. I couldn't read Latin. My high school education didn't include it. A couple years of French, but nothing on the necklace looked remotely close.

"What did that gypsy say?" I wracked my brain, trying to remember. "Something about once back to the beginning. I don't want to be a baby again." Maybe if I thought about when I wanted to be, I'd be there. This was crazy. No way was this thing really gonna work. But I was curious enough to try. I twirled the gold pendant. It caught the light, much like the prism Phillip had brought back for me from one of his trips to Ithaca. It now hung in my window. It was pretty cool.

"Once back to the beginning." I twirled the pendant. Was that even what I was supposed to say? The object did nothing but spin in my hand. She mentioned something about the circle. No, it couldn't be right because this was oval shaped. There was something else, too. Something about a crossroads of heartache maybe? Yeah, that sounded right. Oh heck, I didn't remember. I threw the pendant onto the carpet. I hadn't paid attention to the gypsy's bogus mumble jumble. Now I wish I had. Just so I could see if it worked.

I always liked time travel books. What if I could be a time travel phenomenon like Dr. Who?

I picked up the pendant and tried again to remember what I was supposed to say. Why hadn't I ever gone to the library to look up the meaning of this thing? And the meaning of the Latin writing.

"Okay. The crossroads that broke my heart." Or maybe Henry's heart. But was it really broken after all? "Once back and.....and never again?" No, it was more like, "only use it once and always a way home."

The pendant radiated a glowing light in my hands.

My heart pounded in my chest. Had I activated it? Did I say the right words?

I kept chanting what I could remember, ignoring the knocking on the front door downstairs. Phillip was in the kitchen. He'd answer whoever it was. Probably a vacuum cleaner salesman with a free six pack of Pepsi if we let him clean our carpets. That scam had been going around the neighborhood.

"Once back to the beginning and always a way home." The pendant spun faster and glowed a bright light, illuminating the walls of my dully painted grey walls.

"Awesome!" I repeated the words and concentrated on graduation day before I ran into Henry on the walkway to the reception hall. "The... something ends where it..." Why couldn't I remember that part?

The pendant's spinning slowed. "No!" I recited the words again, but it didn't move. The gypsy said I could only use it once. Was that it? Was that my chance?

A knock at my bedroom door aggravated my already frustrated mood. "Go away! I'm busy!"

"Emelia?" It was Phillip. "Are you okay?"

My heart fell. I assumed it was Alexis at my door. "I'm okay. Sorry. Just...changing."

"Okay. Well, you have company. Would you like me to send him up?"

Him? Henry? Had he come home for a visit?

"No. No. I'll be right down. Have him wait in the living room Phillip."

"All right."

I heard him descend the stairs while I went to my Clairol lighted makeup mirror and turned the dial to evening. I wanted to fix my makeup so I looked good for Henry. He hadn't seen me in more than six months. I didn't want to look like the little girl he left behind for college. He'd spent time with sophisticated girls, smart girls, and most likely beautiful rich girls. I didn't have time to curl my hair, so I teased it with my comb a little bit and applied lots of hair spray to hold it in place. I stepped back and assessed my outfit. It was okay. Jordache jeans and a white off the shoulder sweatshirt. Good enough.

I bounded down the stairs and saw Phillip's back at the entryway to the living room. He talked about the problem with litter on our street. McDonald's foam cartons. He hated those. I couldn't see who he spoke to because his broad shoulders blocked the entryway. I went around through the kitchen to the other door into the living room. My cheeks warmed and my smile stretched out across my face. I didn't even care I smiled like an idiot. I was not going to stop myself from running into Henry's arms to give him a hug. No time to be embarrassed. Maybe the time twister had worked after all by bringing Henry to me. Maybe that's how the thing worked. I didn't go back in time, silly. Time was brought back to me through Henry.

I about fell through the entryway into the living room where I saw Phillip's face this time, still talking to Henry. My clumsy entrance drew Phillip's attention to me, as well as the man he spoke to. The face turned to me and smiled, a bouquet of roses in his hands.

That face.
Not Henry's.
Jasper.

10

The Misunderstanding

"Jasper, what are you doing here?"

Phillip left us alone and went back to the kitchen, most likely to continue his daily crossword puzzle. I heard the buzz of his hearing aid and hoped he was turning it down and not up. I just didn't want him to hear what would definitely be an awkward conversation between Jasper and me.

"Babe. These are for you." Jasper handed the roses to me. I wanted to smash them onto the carpet and stomp on them the way he'd stomped on my heart. He was a total scumbag. But the flowers were pretty and they'd done nothing to me.

"Okay. I have them. Now leave." I pointed to the front door and spoke in a quiet, calm voice so Phillip didn't overhear. He had an old baseball bat at the side of his bed and I didn't want to give him a reason to use it. Not that he would, but he'd threatened to use it on my dad plenty of times if he showed his face around our house. He'd said he didn't like the way my dad treated my mom. So, yeah.

"You don't mean that baby." Jasper took my hands in his. I tried to pull them from him, but he grabbed tighter. "Listen to me, will you?" He looked at me with his big blue eyes. His ocean blue bedroom eyes. My resolve melted away. For some reason, against my conscious will and determination, I wanted to look into those beautiful eyes. And that's when he must have realized he had me back under his spell. He smiled. "I was a prick. A total prick. I won't make that mistake again."

"So, you admit you cheated on me?"

"Hell no. I didn't do anything like that." He narrowed his eyes. "I meant the way I let you walk out of my life. I should have chased after you. I should have taken you into my arms and kissed your beautiful, soft lips." He leaned in at that moment and kissed me.

I pulled away. He was full of something and it wasn't remorse. "Nothing's changed. If you can't apologize for it, much less admit it, there's nothing left to say. Why did you come here? To mess with my head?" Breathing became labored and I struggled for air. Calm the frick down, Emelia. Don't have a cow in front of Jasper.

"Emelia, you have an overactive imagination. I never cheated on you. Where did you get a crazy idea like that?" His eyes pleaded for an answer. No doubt he was using his salesman trickery on me, forcing me to see things *his* way.

"The ashtray. That girl asking me if we could still be friends and apologizing to me for no apparent reason." My heart began to race and bile rose into my throat.

"Emelia, I already explained. Those were mine. I tried a different brand, that's all."

"The girl."

"I'm not going through all that again. Are you going to let something like that come between us?"

"Your boss's girlfriend acted weird. Like she'd done something wrong. I don't even know her. I never met her before that night. She apologized and asked me to be her friend. What the frick, Jasper?"

"What are you talking about? You're making that up."

"No. I'm. Not." I stomped my foot in frustration.

"Look, you're trying to confuse me." He looked directly into my eyes. I could feel the tension as he willed me to listen to him. "Think about when you didn't remember things correctly last time."

"What last time?" Confusion and self-doubt started to dull my brain. I held the sides of my head.

"The night of the office Christmas party? Remember? The one I brought you to." The demand to obey was clear in his voice. "The one where you came into my office looking for me? Cindy was on her knees by my desk and you thought she was doing something

obscene to me. It turned out to be a misunderstanding.
You saw it all wrong. She was just picking up some
money she'd dropped."

Oh yeah. I remembered Cindy. She was the
young single mom that was always broke. Jasper had
told me she sometimes borrowed money from their boss.
That time, Jasper had lent her some money before I
walked in.

"You thought I was cheating that time too, and
you were wrong." His tone was convincing. "Don't you
think you're letting your imagination run wild again?"

Maybe. Maybe he was right. I don't know. I could
be wrong. I'm usually wrong. Jasper often told me I had
a tendency to over-exaggerate. Cindy had always been
good to everyone in the office. And she worked hard to
take care of her kid.

"I don't know Jasper. It was all too weird." A
huge headache banged inside my head. I rubbed my
temples. It was too hard to think. What he was saying
didn't add up. It was like shoving a piece of a puzzle into
the wrong place - it just didn't fit.

"Well, you obviously never believed in me." His
voice was filled with accusation. Guilt rushed in like a
raging river through a busted dam. "You see everything
in the most negative way. And your self-esteem is way
too low. I..." He ran his hand over his chin and stroked
his five o'clock shadow.

Goosebumps tingled my arms, and not because I
was cold. "I believed in you. Believed in us." Why did I

always have to explain myself to him? How did this get turned around on me? "But... why do things like this keep happening, Jasper?" Confusion gripped my mind into a vice.

"Are you trying to hurt me on purpose? I care about you. Did you ever really love me?"

"Oh Jasper, you know I did." I whispered, remembering Phillip was in the next room.

"Why can't you stop nagging me about this and move on. The past is in the past."

"Jasper, do you love me?"

"If I say I love you, you'll expect more out of me. All I have to give is what I'm offering you right now. I can't predict the future. I care about you very much. I'm here aren't I?" He pulled me into his arms. "Let me show you how much I care." He stroked my head and I leaned into his warm chest. His worn blue flannel shirt comforted me. I had missed this. Us. "Can you just get over it, please?" He pulled back and looked into my eyes.

He had come all this way to apologize. Wait, was there an apology in there somewhere? I didn't remember. He'd said a lot of things, like he'd cared. He brought flowers, which he'd never done in the past. That had to count for something, right? I sighed into his chest and kissed the exposed skin covered in blond, wiry hairs. "Yes, Jasper." I whispered softly. He kissed me fiercely and leaned into me with his firm body.

"Got anything going on? Maybe we could go see a movie."

"I suppose..." He cut me off before I could finish. "If you don't want to, I get it. I probably interrupted something." He looked towards the stairway to where my bedroom was. He thrust his hands into his pockets and jingled the change inside. "Were you hanging out with that queer friend of yours?" At my look of confusion, he added, "Henry?" He spoke quietly, but there was no mistaking his tone of voice. Jealousy.

"No. Henry isn't here."

"Another guy then?" His hands balled into fists in his pockets. I could count every knuckle on his hands through his faded blue jeans. "I'm sure you didn't waste any time." His voice was a low growl, barely audible, intended for my ears alone.

"Of course not, Jasper. It's not like it's been that long since we broke up."

"Were we broke up? We had a fight. So, if I'd waited a few days longer, you would have whored around with someone else?"

"Jasper!" I kept my voice quiet so as not to get Phillip involved. But Jasper's voice had been intimidatingly loud. "I wouldn't do that." Tears threatened to pour onto my cheeks. Hadn't we made up? Why would he call me something so awful? Did I dress in a way that made me come off as easy? Was it the way I acted around him that made him think that about me? I hung my head, ashamed.

"I wasn't here. How would I know?" He took my hand in his. "Let's go."

"Jasp, I need to get my jacket. My purse." I pulled my hand from his as Phillip entered the living room with his arms across his chest.

"Sure, Emelia. Go ahead." He returned Phillip's glare and let go of my hand. "I'll wait in the car."

I ran upstairs to grab my jacket and purse off my bed. When I turned to leave, the glimmer of the time traveling pendant caught my eye. I kicked it under my bed. "Stupid thing doesn't work anyways." It had conjured the wrong guy.

I heard the roar of Jasper's Nova and hurried down the stairs two steps at a time. Andrea appeared at the bottom of the steps. "Got a second, Emelia?"

"Not really. Jasper's waiting for me." I slid my arms into my jacket and pulled my purse strap over my shoulder.

"Just a minute." She held up one finger.

"But Jasper..."

"He can wait one minute, right?" Her gaze was intense, as though she searched my soul for something.

I swallowed hard at the thickness in my throat. "Of course he can."

She wrapped her arms around me and gave me a hug. "I love you so much. You're such a great big sister."

"Thanks. I love you too." I gave her a quick hug and tried to pull away, a little confused at her random affection.

She looked into my eyes, seriousness on her face. "Why do you put up with that?"

"With what?" I shrugged.

"Jasper. All that stuff he said to you. It didn't even make any sense to me. It's like..." She looked upwards and tugged on her golden curls. "It made my head hurt."

"I didn't know you heard any of that. You shouldn't eavesdrop." I couldn't look her in the eyes. Apparently, I wasn't the only one confused.

"I didn't mean to. I just did. And then I couldn't stop because I was trying to figure it all out." She raised and dropped her hands in exasperation.

"Andrea, you're just too young to understand how relationships work."

"Maybe. But I *am* old enough to know that you are smart. If you believe something is true, I believe you too."

"You're sweet." She was too young to really understand. "I gotta run. I'll see you later, okay?"

"Sure." She stepped aside to let me pass. "Have fun."

The car door was heavy, a little off track since Jasper's accident, and it took both hands to pull on the door handle to get it open. The front end was buckled like an accordion from his accident. He'd fallen asleep at the wheel on his way home from one of his out-of-town meetings and hit a telephone pole. Luckily, he hadn't been hurt. But the front end of the car threw off the entire frame and now the doors were jacked up. He'd had a few months in a row of low sales volume and couldn't afford to get it fixed yet.

"About freaking time!" I didn't have the car door closed before he burned rubber away from the curb.

"Sorry. Just saying good-bye to Andrea." I groped for something to hang on to.

"It's not like you don't see her everyday!" He pressed down on the gas pedal as he took the turn. I slid on the seat and smooshed my face up against the window.

"What the frick! You trying to kill us?" I reached for my seatbelt, but it was tucked way down in the seat. I pulled, but was met with resistance. It was caught on something inside the seat.

He laughed. "I know what I'm doing. I drive all the time." He hit the brakes on the next turn and I slid onto the floor.

"That's it." I reached for the door handle and pushed against the heavy piece of crap, trying to open it so I could jump out. Jasper sped up and turned sharply to the left, which had me in his lap. He wrapped his arm around me.

"I wanted to have you sit next to me. That's all." He kissed the top of my head. "I like having you next to me."

"Oh. Well, all you had to do was ask." I straightened myself and ran a hand thru my tussled hair in an attempt to get it out of my eyes. What was with his mood swings tonight?

He laughed. "I'm asking now."

I nuzzled my head into his neck.

"I missed you." Jasper pulled to the side of the dark, country road we were on.

"I missed you too." I looked out the window into darkness and the black woods. My imagination dreamed up creatures that could be prowling around in the dark right now. There were no stars. No moon. Only dark clouds. The billowy kind that hung low and didn't budge to let the moon shine her light. Just because I couldn't see the moon and the stars shining didn't mean they weren't up there, hidden behind the darkness. "What are you doing?"

Jasper put his lips on mine. His mustache tickled my lips.

"Jasp..."

"Shhh." He put his lips to mine again. I kissed him back, because he had that effect on me. He made me forget what I was going to say. His lips moved across my neck and to my ears where he nibbled on my lobe. I could hear the sound of my earring post clank against his teeth. I giggled when he blew into my ear.

"That tickles." I pulled away, but he pulled me back to him. "Jasper. What about the movie?" I tried to read my watch. It was too dark and my other hand couldn't reach the indiglo button to light it up.

"We'll catch the later show." He mumbled the words into my ear while he touched me on top of my shirt.

"Uhh. I can't stay out late."

He smiled against my lips. "Sure you can. You're a big girl."

"Yeah, but I have an early shift at Fly Buyz tomorrow." I pushed his hand from where it had roamed and landed it back onto my waist.

Jasper snorted. "Call off."

"Jasp. I can't afford to do that. I'm saving for college."

"What do you need college for?" His brows lowered.

"I don't want to work at a grocery store forever." I wanted to get out of my parent's house someday soon. I wanted a real career and a home all my own. And Muffin, along with a lot of other cats.

"C'mon Emelia." Jasper reached around under the back of my shirt to my bra strap.

"Stop, Jasper." I pushed my back against the seat of the car, forcing him to remove his hand. "We just got back together." Why did he always act like nothing had happened between us? How could he just pick up where we left off like there was never anything wrong?

"Hey. We got back together that night at dinner. The rest was just a misunderstanding." He moved his hand over the front of my shirt again.

I stopped that move. "No, Jasper. I don't think we should do that." I wanted to think with a clear mind, and not be distracted by my hormones. Or Jasper's.

He laughed. "Do *that?*"

"I don't want you to touch me like that."

"You make me sound like poison potatoes." He had a trace of humor to his voice.

I moved away from him, my resolve firm. "I don't think it's a good idea. We should talk to my pastor and get some advice from him." I hadn't been to church much since dating Jasper. With his work hours, we could only get together on weekends, mostly on Sundays.

He crossed his arms. "I am not doing that. Crap, Emelia, you know the church broke up my first marriage."

"It was a cult, so it doesn't count." Jehovah Witnesses were close enough to being a cult in my opinion.

"It was not." His voice didn't sound convincing.

"Um, I'm pretty sure it was. They spied on your house to see if you had a Christmas tree. And presents. All pretty weird. No Christmas or Easter? You couldn't even celebrate your birthday. Totally lame."

He stared out the windshield into the darkness. I wondered if I'd brought up bad memories for him. Like his little girl he didn't see often since he'd moved an hour away from here, and she was another hour east from me. He could have been with his daughter tonight, but he chose to be with me. I'm not sure how that made me feel. A little sad, actually. Little girls need their dads. Mine didn't really care if I lived or died, but I had Phillip and that was better than nothing, most of the time anyways. Jasper should be with his daughter. The three-year-old little girl who never celebrated her birthday, and would never remember the Christmas tree her dad had put up for her first Christmas. But after his church 'deacons', and I use the word totally loosely, had peeked into his family's windows and spotted the glittering lights and tinsel, they'd disfellowshipped them all. Jasper had told me his ex-wife denounced him in order to get her and their daughter back in good standing with their church. I guess I was being insensitive and should drop the subject.

"So, The Toy or Tootsie?" I asked Jasper, trying to bring him back to the present.

"What are you talking about?" His tone was distant and I wondered where his thoughts were.

"Those are the movies at the Palace theatre."

"I don't care." He started the car and headed back towards the city. "You pick one."

11

Technicolor Dreams

Movie night was not even fun. Jasper slept thru two thirds of Tootsie. Dustin Hoffman in drag was rad. It's funny to see butt-ugly men dress as women. Jasper doesn't find them as funny as I do. I found that out when *Bosom Buddies* aired. I couldn't get him interested in cross dressing humor. That Tom Hanks, though. I had a good feeling he'd be a big splash in Hollywood.

I didn't get my dinner either. I was super hungry when I got home. I grabbed the loaf of Millbrook bread, my sisters and I called it *Snoopy bread* since his picture was on the bag, piled it with chunky peanut butter and grape jelly, and took it to my room. It calmed my rumbling belly. Jasper had been quick to get me home so he could drive back to Erie and get some sleep. That's what he'd told me, anyways.

Our reunion had not been so romantic. It was totally anti-climactic. But Jasper had walked me to the door and kissed me goodnight before he'd left. He apologized for sleeping through the movie and insisted he'd make it up to me next weekend. We'd see about that. He rarely came through on his promises.

I loved Jasper to the Milky Way and beyond, but I was still raw from our fight a while back and something still nagged at my gut. And that something wasn't right. But I would do whatever it took to make our relationship work. Love was about sacrifice and compromise. I could change for Jasper if I needed to.

Yawning, I set my plate on the rug next to my bed and climbed under the covers without even brushing my teeth. I was so tired, I started to dream before I fell asleep. My dreams were as vivid as technicolor vomit. I was at Uncle Pips playing foosball with some of the regulars and I really kicked butt. It was cold, snowy, and Johnny's pizza oven was filled with pizza subs for all the kids that hung out that night. He called it a snowstorm special. I knew it was definitely a dream because Johnny was cheap. He wouldn't have given away the ending to a book, he was so cheap. The door opened and a gust of wind and snow blew into the room and sent shivers up and down my arms. I was behind the wall that separated the entrance from the game room side of the small teenage hangout. I couldn't see who had walked in. The room was dimly lit, but whoever walked in illuminated the room. The Langworthy twins kept playing and scored on me twice while I stared towards the entrance to see who had come in.

"C'mon Emelia. Get your head in the game," Alan Langworthy chided me.

"Yeah, I'm going to get a soda." I walked away from my goalie position and the ball scored on our team.

Alan and Trevor moaned, but I knew they'd wait for me. It's like everything in this dream moved in slow motion. I walked towards the snack counter, my feet weightless. I couldn't feel the floor beneath them. My strides took great effort, like walking in water. The closer I got to the counter, the brighter the light and the harder to see. I shielded my eyes with my hand. I was close to the figure. It was a tall form of a man glowing around the edges of a dark shadow. It stood at the counter talking to Johnny who smiled at the man, or woman, in the brightness of their own light.

I heard the voice, familiar and soothing. Did I know this person? Was this an afterlife experience? Oh Lord! I hadn't been to church since last summer. I was going to hell.

But when the face turned towards me, it wasn't the face of God. It was the face of Henry.

"Emelia. Find me." His voice came out in a creepy science-fiction movie type of high squeal. Like an alien. He stretched out his arms and his expression pleaded with me.

My skin goose pimpled at his words and I awoke in a puddle of my own sweat.

12

Camera Shy

I tried to call Jasper several times on Saturday to make sure he got home okay. He never answered. Kelli-Anne called me first thing in the morning to see if I wanted to do lunch and some shopping. I was hesitant to say yes or no until I knew if Jasper would make another surprise visit. The last time I wasn't home when he drove out to see me, it didn't end well. He'd been very angry and I guess I always screwed up things anyways. I wanted to be better so Jasper wouldn't get mad at me. So we wouldn't fight again. I could do better and try harder for sure.

After the fifth try, I called Kelli-Anne.

"I'm gonna have to pass this time, Kelli-Anne. I haven't heard from Jasper and I don't want to miss his call."

"That's okay. How 'bout I stop over? I'll bring some fries and Cokes from McDonalds. We can chill in your room and catch up. Or if you want to, we can watch MTV."

I laughed. "Your dad still have you on the antenna?"

She moaned, "Yeeeees. Three channels of nothing on. Do you guys have HBO?"

"No. Mom and Phillip didn't spring for that luxury, but we do have the 13 cable channels. We'll find something to watch. And thanks for understanding."

"Of course. I miss you. I wanted to hang out and have some girl talk."

"Everything okay with James?" She'd dated him since eleventh grade, the same year I met Jasper. We were best friends in high school, but had drifted apart once we had boyfriends. We didn't get to spend as much time together anymore.

"Yeah. I need some girl time. My brothers are driving me nuts and James is out of town visiting his grandma with his family this weekend."

I can't imagine having four brothers. Two older, two younger, and all were big tormentors. Poor Kelli-Anne was stuck in the middle of a freak show. "Well, there's plenty of girls around here. So I'll see you around what time?"

"About 12:30. Does that sound good?"

"Yep. See you."

After our good-byes I ran up the steps to my room. I didn't have much time to clean with everything going on last week. I stood in the doorway and assessed the damage. The plate and glass from last night's bedtime snack still sat next to my bed along with the half-empty bag of corn chips. Not too bad. I ran my finger along my dresser and pulled it away to find a thin layer of grey fuzz. Ugh! I'd have to dust. I put away the few items of clothing laid over my desk chair and carried the dishes to the kitchen.

The house would need vacuumed. Everyone was out this morning, so I wouldn't be bothered and could finish quickly. Mom might even be impressed I'd cleaned when it was Andrea's turn this week.

I looked at my watch after putting away the cleaning supplies. I had a half hour to grab a shower and wash my hair. I was grody from cleaning.

Kelli-Anne rang my door bell at exactly 12:30 and I opened the door to see her in a blue parka, the hood pulled tight around her curly brown hair. "Wow! C'mon in." I stepped aside so she could come in out of the blowing snow. "When did the storm start?" I took the bag and drink tray from her so she could pull off her boots and coat.

"About an hour ago. You didn't know?" She shook her head to prevent hat hair.

"No, I haven't looked out the window in a while. Let's sit in the living room, it's warmer than my bedroom." The heat seemed to disappear in the heating ducts before it made its way up to my room.

The fries were super salty and the Cokes sweet; a perfect combination on a cold, snowy afternoon. We turned on MTV and rocked out to *Down Under* and *Man-eater*, sang along with the MTV theme song, and tried to imitate the corpses dancing to Michael Jackson's *Thriller*.

"That song is so awesome!" Kelli-Anne fell back into the gold velvet recliner where my mom liked to do her knitting. "My dad would kill me if he knew I was watching it. Worse, I tried to dance to it." She giggled and took another sip of her Diet Coke.

"What a rush!" I slid onto the floor next to Kelli-Anne. "I hope they play it again so we can work on our moves." I moved my hands like the zombies in the video. "Man, I miss dancing."

"Why don't you dance anymore?"

"Jasper doesn't like to go dancing. Anyways, I guess I've outgrown that phase of my life." Not really. I'd still love to go out and dance until the clubs closed. The last time I'd gone was with friends. Jasper was so mad at me for going out with them, he'd accused me of all sorts of heinous things. I'd promised him I wouldn't go out to the clubs anymore.

She nodded slowly. "How is Jasper? I haven't seen him since, like, ever. He wasn't at graduation, was he?"

"No. He had work out of town. That was a crazy day. I don't think I saw you at all."

"I saw you." She took a long drink of her Diet Coke and burped. We laughed. It was funny to hear such a loud noise come out of her tiny body. She was four feet and eleven inches of sass and spunk.

"Why didn't you say something?" I threw one last fry in my mouth and savored the salt on my tongue. It tasted better than anything I'd eaten in quite some time.

She held her straw between her teeth and seemed to replay the moment in her mind before she said anything. "It looked like you were talking about something important."

"At the reception? No, just the family talking about nothing much of anything, ya know?"

"Not at the reception, Emelia." She pulled her hair behind her ear. "On the way to the reception. On a bench under a tree." She leaned closer to me, as though we weren't the only two people in the house. "With Henry."

I coughed and Coke sprayed everywhere...onto the carpet, my jeans, the chair. I fought to get my breath back after I gagged on the syrupy drink. Kelli-Anne *had* seen me with Henry. Who else, I wondered, had seen us? I hope nobody that knew Jasper. Jasper didn't like Henry and made it no secret to either of us. He'd be pissed to hear Henry had tried to kiss me.

"Sorry. I didn't mean to say anything wrong. It seemed like a very private moment and I didn't want to interrupt. And I guess that's why I wondered about Jasper. I hope I didn't say something to upset you."

Kelli-Anne couldn't upset an applecart. "It's fine."

"I don't think anyone else saw you."

"It wasn't a big deal. We were just saying good-bye before he went off to college. A private good-bye before we got to the busy reception."

She snorted. "Emelia, it's me, your best friend. I know we haven't had a lot of time together since junior year, but we can pick up where we left off whether it's been two days or two years."

I nodded. She was right. Being with her was more natural than being with my own flesh and blood sisters.

"You two seemed very serious. And he was so close to you, it looked like he would kiss you." She quickly shook her head. "Don't worry. I never told anybody."

What might Jasper say if he knew? I swallowed against the ball forming in my throat. "It wouldn't have mattered. Nothing happened. But Kelli-Anne, something *almost* did."

She nodded, stood, and stretched. "When are your parents coming home?"

I shrugged. "They are at a Lion's Club fundraiser. Collecting glasses or bowling. I'm not sure which." It was sad I didn't know a thing about my parent's activities.

"Alexis and Andrea?"

"I think they're helping out with the fundraiser." I wasn't sure about that either, because Alexis always found a way to get out of it.

"Are you sure we're alone?" She held a finger to her lips and pointed to the stairway hidden by a dividing wall.

I winked. "Absolutely." I took my cue and tip-toed over to the bottom of the stairs. I poked my head around the corner and roared like a waking lion.

"Bitch!" Alexis wrapped her robe around her and turned to go up the stairs. I grabbed the hem and tugged her back down the two steps she'd taken. "Let me go!"

"C'mon in and join us, Alexis We have some fries left." How long had she been listening? Not that we'd talked about anything important. We'd mostly acted like dorks, dancing embarrassingly around the living room.

She turned and stood akimbo. "I am not hungry. Now, let me go."

"Why? You kinda look like you wanted to be down here with us." I fake smiled at her, hiding my irritation.

She pursed her lips and tapped her foot. "I'm telling Jasper what you did."

My heart pounded so hard, I'm sure Alexis heard it. She smiled like a predator, ear-to-ear, with all her teeth bared.

"Alexis, I was saying that stuff because I knew you were listening." Kelli-Anne stood at the bottom of the stairs now, a Hershey bar extended towards Alexis. Aw, her Achilles heel. Chocolate.

I swear I saw Alexis lick her lips in anticipation of the savory chocolate. "Naw, ah. I heard Emelia say something almost happened. Jasper is so gonna kill you, Emelia." She smiled like the Cheshire cat.

"You bought that?" Kelli-Anne laughed. She held her belly for effect. "Man, you're easy." She handed her the candy bar which quickly disappeared into the fluffy pockets of infinity. "We both knew you were standing there. We saw your shadow and were messing with you."

Alexis raised an eyebrow, and tugged her robe out of my hand. "You owe me, Emelia." She looked towards the ceiling for a few seconds and snapped her fingers. "Buy me a pack of cigarettes and I won't tell."

"Alexis, omigod, I just can't even...."

"Here," Kelli-Anne handed her a dollar. "You can walk to the store and buy your own cigarettes." She reached into her pocket and handed her another dollar. "And you can have a Coke and another candy bar on me." Alexis reached for the money, but my spunky little friend held on tight. "You have to promise not to cause trouble for Emelia first." Kelli-Anne squinted her eyes, trying to look tough.

"Fine." Alexis snatched the money, ran upstairs to her room, and slammed the door shut. I heard it lock. With any luck, she'd get dressed and leave. Maybe she'd get lost in a snow bank on the way back.

"Why don't we go to your room and turn up the music loud so we can have a real girl talk."

"Good idea." I led the way to my room.

Muffin jumped off my bed to greet Kelli-Anne. She rubbed her legs and did a figure eight around them.

Kelli-Anne rubbed her head in return. Muffin seemed satisfied with the attention. She jumped back onto my bed, curled into a ball, and went back to sleep.

I locked my bedroom door in case Alexis snuck up on us again. Alexis would hold what she'd overheard against me for eternity. Nothing had happened I should be ashamed of. I'd turned Henry down, although now I wish I hadn't. Where did that thought come from? No, I didn't mean it. I loved... love Jasper. And why did I want to find Henry?

Because I missed him. Because when Jasper was a major prick or I had a fight with my mom, Henry was the one person I wanted to talk to about it. Not Kelli-Anne or Phillip. Not even Andrea. I wanted to talk to Henry. And he always seemed to be around at the right moment, when I needed him most.

I put the *Eagles Long Run* album on the turntable and cranked the volume to about half-way. It was loud enough to cover our voices, but not so loud we couldn't hear each other.

"So, give me the scoop." Kelli-Anne fell down into the bean bag chair, which wasn't a long fall for her petite legs. I wish the seat worked as well for me.

"It's nothing really. And you can't say anything. Alexis is right about one thing, Jasper would be mad at me whether it's true or not?"

"What happened with Henry?"

"Nothing. Really, I didn't let it."

"Jasper shouldn't be angry with you. Maybe he should be mad at Henry, but he's off at college."

"Yeah, about that. He never registered."

"How do you know that?" Kelli-Anne leaned forward in the bean bag chair.

"I called. He's not there. They have his application and acceptance letter, but he never showed." She smiled. "You called?"

"Well, of course. I tried finding his number around his birthday too, and there wasn't one listed. He's my friend, after all."

"And that's all there is to it?" Kelli-Anne eyed me skeptically.

"Yes. I promise. I didn't realize how much I missed him until he wasn't here anymore."

"So what *did* happen that has you all worked up?" She zipped her lips. "And of course I promise not to tell anyone."

We did the whole pinky swear ritual and I told her about the conversation with Henry and the almost kiss that didn't happen. "And that's all there was to it."

"Well, it shouldn't have been a big surprise he'd try it when Jasper wasn't around and he had you to himself."

"We were hardly alone."

"Well, as alone as you would be. No sisters, parents, or boyfriend hanging around. You really didn't suspect anything?" I shook my head. "Honestly, Emelia."

She leaned towards me and hugged me tight. "You are so obtuse."

"What do you mean by that?" My entire face tightened.

"Emelia, anyone could see he looked at you as more than a friend. And the way you two acted when you were together." She sighed. "It was so natural. I'd see him waiting at your locker every morning before school. I asked him a few times what he was doing. *Oh, just waiting for Emelia. I need help with a homework question.* Or after school, he wanted to see if you got the homework assignments for math because he wasn't listening or couldn't hear in the back of the room."

"So? Those are legit reasons. He really did have questions. And he struggled with math."

"He's a genius at math, Emelia."

"No." I hesitated. "He asked for help. I helped him with his essays. And his college admissions essay. And I helped with his algebra and geometry too." I laughed at the memory. "He always struggled in math."

Kelli-Anne shook her head. "He was in my class. He always knew the answers to the problems on the board. He didn't need help, Emelia. He needed an excuse to see *you*."

"No. That can't be it. We were friends. *Just* friends."

"Well that's what he wanted you to think. I bet he was waiting for you and Jasper to break up so he could make his move. But Jasper always lurks around." She moved her hands like they were spiders.

"You make him sound like some kind of stalker." I laughed at the image of Jasper peeking into my second story window.

"Not a stalker, but..." She tapped her chin and didn't finish her thought. "Anyways, I guess Henry had to make a move on graduation day, knowing it might be the last time he'd see you."

My heart grew heavy in my chest. Maybe it had been the last time I'd see Henry.

Kelli-Anne put a hand on my shoulder. "Don't worry. He'll be back."

"Jasper?"

"No. Henry."

"I don't think so. If what you're saying is true..."

"It is Emelia. Omigod, it was so evident the way he looked at you."

"Ooo kaaaay. Well, let's say it's true. He won't want to see me ever again. I wish I could tell him I'm sorry. I would never have hurt him on purpose."

"What do you imagine would have happened that day? If he'd landed that kiss."

"I haven't a clue. Maybe I would have slapped him because he knew I had a boyfriend. But maybe what I did was worse than a slap."

"Hmm. You're too hard on yourself. He has to know you were caught off guard." She looked behind me. "What's that?"

"What's what?" I turned to where she looked. Did I miss a pair of dirty socks or a shirt?

She knelt next to my bed and pulled out a shiny object. "This? It's very interesting. And sparkly." She held it by its chain and the light reflected off its golden surface. Why did that thing keep resurfacing?

"It's some kind of time travel portal." Sarcasm flowed from my lips.

"Ooh. Is it a souvenir from the science museum?" She inspected the shiny gold filigree.

"No. I got it from that gypsy fortune teller last summer at the Gala Days."

"The fortune teller that disappeared before I could meet her?" I nodded. "That was odd." She rubbed her jaw. "You never told me she gave you this."

"I was too busy tripping over my own feet, remember?" I did that a lot. Tripped over my freakishly huge feet.

Kelli-Anne giggled. "I remember. Well, it's pretty. How come you never wear it?"

"I don't know. Maybe because it's not very stylish."

She put it over her neck. "I don't know. It's cool. If you don't want it, I'll keep it."

"I want it. I just don't want to wear it."

"Okay." She took it off and handed it to me, but she still admired the sparkly pendant.

I wouldn't wear it, but I did think it was cool. Creepy, but cool just the same. "I tried it out to see if it worked."

Kelli-Anne jerked her head back. "What'd it do?"

"It spun around, but I think it moved because I'd held it up. Or maybe a breeze made it move."

"You open your windows in January?" She gave me a scrutinizing look.

"Well, maybe it was the air through the heating duct. Either way, it didn't work."

"Where would you have gone, Emelia?"

I wasn't sure I should say. "Well, since it was just in fun, I tried to go back to graduation day, right before Henry and I sat under the tree."

She grinned. "Ooh. So, you have had second thoughts about not kissing him?"

"Only fleeting. I mean, when I couldn't find him, I tried calling the colleges and information, but nobody knew anything. I gave it a try. I was an emotional teenager, right?" I fingered the delicate etching on the outside of the necklace.

"I don't know. I've never known you to be overly emotional."

"Maybe not. Maybe I just wondered how things could have been different from what they are."

"Can we try it now?" Kelli-Anne eyed the necklace like Gollum eyed the ring in the *Lord of the Rings* books. *My Precious.* I doubted she'd ever read the *Lord of the Rings* trilogy. She was more into romantic books. Gag me! Give me fantasy or science fiction any day over that.

"I don't care. Where do you want to go?" I sat cross-legged on the floor next to her.

"Well, does it take you anywhere you want to go?"

"It hasn't taken me anywhere." I laughed. "This is purely speculative, right?"

"Yeah, sure. I meant how far back can you go, theoretically? And can you go to the future? That would be cool, to see the future. Our futures."

"No, it doesn't go forward." I remembered the gypsy's words, *once back*. "Only back in time. I don't know why it works that way, but that's what the lady said."

"Hmm." She tapped her chin, eyes closed in deep concentration. "We could go back to the first day of sophomore year. That was a fun time. But, will we be ourselves back at that time, or will we be back there with ourselves from the past?"

"Good question. I never thought of that."

"That could be a problem. I mean, if I run into myself, I won't be freaked out because I'm expecting it, but the me from the past would totally freak out, I'm sure."

"Good point." I rested the pendant in my hand, and covered it with the other. If I could only use it once, if it really did work, I wanted to go find Henry. "Maybe we should look into it more before using it."

"Sure. We definitely need to know more." Kelli-Anne pulled a Polaroid out of her massively large macrame purse and held it over my hands. "Let me take a picture of it. I can check at the library and see if there are any books with information on it."

Kelli-Anne was pretty good at research for school papers, so I opened my hands and let her take a picture. She waved it in the air while it developed, and slowly the picture went from black to green to the color of flesh. My hand. The pendant wasn't visible on the photo. "You must not have centered the camera over it."

"Weird? I thought I had." Kelli-Anne looked at the front of the camera, like that would make a difference. "I must have had my finger in front of the viewer. Let me try again."

I held the necklace towards the little bit of light that shone through the window for a better shot. It still snowed. It reflected its own bit of light, but the sun hid behind the clouds.

Again, she took a picture of the pendant and we waited for the film to develop.

She held it up so I could see. "Nothing. I don't understand." She took a picture of Muffin, who was asleep at the bottom of my bed. It slowly developed into a perfectly clear picture of my black and white cat on the green and yellow comforter of my bed. "That's so freaky."

"Maybe it's camera shy?" I laughed, but not at all amused. This object might very well be cursed. I should let Kelli-Anne have it. She wanted it and I totally didn't want to be around it anymore. "Here, you can take it with you and research it if you want." I placed it in her hand.

"Okay. I guess so." She seemed reluctant to take it now, like maybe it freaked her out a little bit too, but neither of us wanted to be the one to admit it.

Over the lyrics of *Heartache Tonight,* we both jumped to the banging on my bedroom door.

"Go away Alexis. You got your extortion money. Go buy your own cigarettes." I laughed and Kelli-Anne shook her head. She thought she had it bad with brothers. Cakewalk.

"It's not Alexis."

The deep voice was certainly not Alexis or Phillip.

Kelli-Anne and I stared at each other, neither one moved. The banging on my door was louder the second time. "What are you hiding, Emelia?"

Jasper. His voice. Alexis let him in without telling me he was here. It was her passive-aggressive way of getting even with me for earlier.

Kelli-Anne hid the pendant in her purse, as if Jasper was here for that. I had barely turned the lock when he bulldozed his way into my room. He looked towards the bed first and completely overlooked Kelli-Anne. He glared at me for a good fifteen seconds before Kelli-Anne cleared her throat. "Well, I guess I'll head home now."

"No, don't leave." I pleaded with my eyes in hopes she'd get the message. I did not want to be alone with Jasper right now. His face reddened at my words.

Jasper went to the stereo and scratched the needle across the record to turn it off rather than lift and rest it in its cradle. When his back was to me, I mouthed, *Please don't go* to Kelli-Anne, but she mouthed back *I'm sorry. Gotta run.* That was the moment I remembered she always left when Jasper was around. He always seemed to pick that time to be in a bad mood. Actually, it seemed he was in a bad mood when any of my friends or family were around.

She gave me a quick hug and whispered, "*I'm going to the library Monday. I'll let you know what I find out about the pendant. If nothing else, we'll have an interesting story to tell.*"

That's more than I deserved. "Thanks for stopping over, Kelli-Anne. We'll do lunch soon."

She nodded and was gone in a flash. As she ran out the door, I saw Alexis grin at me from her bedroom door across the hallway. She pulled a cigarette from her fluffy vault, lit it, and exhaled smoke like the hookah-smoking Caterpillar. She flipped me off, went into her room, and closed the door behind her. She'd left me alone with Jasper.

13

Sisters Before Misters

"I called you a dozen times and you didn't answer the phone. Nobody answered the phone. So, I'm worried something's wrong and drive 65 miles in a snowstorm to check on you only to find your smoking sister lounging in her robe and you locked away in your room, doing God knows what, blasting that awful music of yours." He was finally out of air and inhaled a deep breath.

"First of all, the *Eagles* are awesome, not awful." I teased, hoping to lighten his mood.

Jasper slammed his fist into the wall and glared at me. I jumped, more on the inside than the outside of my body. My flesh crawled and my heart beat so fast, I got a little bit lightheaded. He wasn't kidding around. Muffin jumped off the bed and hissed at him, taking a swing with her paw before she ran out of my room. "Why didn't you answer the phone?" His eyeballs bulged out of his head like my dad's used to do when he was beyond furious and ready to take a swing at me. I shrank back from him.

"It never rang. I waited all morning for you to call. I even called you, but couldn't get a hold of you. I didn't think you'd come out today since you didn't call me."

"You didn't think, is right!"

"Jasp, I've been here with Kelli-Anne. That's all."

"Is it? Is it really Emelia?" His face told me he thought otherwise. If I didn't confess to whatever he thought I was guilty of he'd stay mad, but if I did he might get madder. Besides, I didn't know what I'd be confessing to.

"Yes Jasper. I should have answered the phone when you called." I inched closer, wrapped my arms around his waist, and nuzzled his neck in hopes of calming him. "Maybe you called when I was in the shower. Or vacuuming. So of course I wouldn't have heard it."

His voice didn't waver from the angry tirade he'd started this tete-a-tete out on. "Alexis is home. You probably told her not to answer the phone."

I snorted. "Well, I highly doubt Alexis would do anything I asked her to do."

"What?" He roared.

My nerves jumped and I pulled away from him. "I'm saying she would have answered it double time if I'd told her not to answer it. And I wouldn't do that anyways. I *wanted* to talk to you. I'd been waiting all morning for you. And I did try to call you about half a dozen times. Alexis probably didn't hear the phone either. She's been hiding in her room all day to avoid volunteer work with Mom and Phillip." I stopped talking to catch my breath. Why did I always make him so mad? What's wrong with me?

He stood quiet, his tongue ran along his upper lip. I excused myself to the bathroom and left him with his thoughts. I'd had that large Coke and really needed to go. I also needed to put some distance between Jasper's temper and me right now.

When I got back to my room, he sat on my bed with my blue notebook opened on his lap. Oh no! Oh crap! He wouldn't understand. I'd written a story for fun. A romance for True Story magazine. And I hated romance. But, since I couldn't afford to go to college, I'd keep my writing skills sharp. And maybe sell some stories. People loved those true romance magazines.

"So you're in love with some other guy, huh?" He looked at the pages open in front of him. "You're writing all about it in this notebook you had hidden under your pillow."

I reached for the notebook and tossed it in the corner behind my dresser. "No. That's a story I'm writing." My cheeks warmed and I patted them with my cold hands. I should have been mad at him for invading my privacy. Instead, he'd managed to make me feel guilty.

He shook his head and looked at his feet. "What's going on with you, Emelia? I hate drama." His hands were clenched at his sides. "What you don't understand is I've had a much harder life than you. I've had bad relationships." He rubbed his forehead, head down.

I remembered how his wife had given him up for her religion. But I wasn't her. "I'm so sorry Jasper." I knelt beside him. "I didn't mean to make you angry." I gave his knee a light squeeze.

"If you'd only change, we could be happy and not fight all the time. I hate fighting. But, I don't know." His voice softened. "Maybe it won't work. I don't have time for your games."

Guilt came knocking on my heart again. "I'm not playing games Jasper." I took his hands in mine.

"I'm an easy going guy Emelia. And I'm the best thing that's ever happened to you."

"I know Jasper. I know." I laid my head in his lap. Nobody else would ever want me or love me. My own parents treated me with indifference. I was lucky to have Jasper to put up with me. "Let me make it up to you."

He tilted his head and looked at me. "I don't have to take this, you know. I'm a grown man. Can you please grow up?"

I nodded. I didn't care tears flowed and made my cheeks sticky.

He stroked the top of my head and leaned down to kiss me.

"Uh, hmm." Alexis stood in the doorway of my bedroom. Why hadn't I shut it? How much had she heard?

"What are you doing in my room Alexis?" I went towards the door to slam it in her face. She pushed her hand against it. "Mom and Phillip are home. I thought..." she looked at Jasper, her eyes narrowed, "you should know just in case, well you know." She raised her eyebrows.

"I really don't." I tried to push the door shut to no avail. She must have a lot of weight in those fluffy robe pockets of hers.

"In case you were going to boink."

"Ew! Gross, Alexis."

"Okay, I've gotta book." Jasper pried the door from Alexis. He leaned in to my ear, "And this is the childish crap I was talking about."

"Jasp, please. You don't have to go." I tugged on his shirt sleeve, but he yanked it from me. I pushed Alexis out of the way and followed him down the stairs. "When will I see you again?" Was this the moment I'd finally pushed him away for good?

"I don't know." He never turned around. Never looked at me. He stepped out the front door and headed to his car.

I followed him, called out to him, but he still didn't turn around. A foot of snow had accumulated and I hadn't stopped to put on shoes or slippers. Or my coat. I knocked on his car window. "I said I was sorry." I couldn't help it that Alexis had barged into my room. Why was I always apologizing and screwing up everything?

He rolled the window down a smidgeon. "You're always sorry. Just go inside." Dismissed. I'd been dismissed in the same way Mom always dismissed me.

"Are we okay?" I sniffled and wiped the tears from my cheeks.

"We'll see. I'm not sure what I want anymore. Things might work out and they might not. No promises." I heard the coldness in his voice. The same coldness I lived with every day. Why did I bring out the worst in people?

My head spun. What the heck had happened? Had I lost my mind? We'd made up right, or did I imagine that? None of this made any sense. Today's roller coaster of emotions tore at my soul.

"See ya." He rolled up his window and pulled off. Snow accumulated on my arms as I stood there alone, barefoot in the snow. Tears flowed down my cheeks. I rubbed my eyes to find black eyeliner and mascara smeared on my fists.

My stomach did its usual as I ran back towards the house. I didn't make it indoors before I barfed, tainting the perfect new-fallen snow. I ruined its beauty like I ruined everything in my life.

"What were you doing outdoors without a coat?" Mom and Phillip sat in the living room, sharing the newspaper, comfortable and normal. A normal life, while mine was a train-wreck. Why couldn't Jasper and I be like them? "And no boots either?" Mom added. I looked at my bright red feet.

"I was in a hurry and forgot to grab them." I rubbed my feet on the carpet, creating friction to hopefully take away the numbness. "Jasper had to go."

"What was he doing out in this weather in the first place? This is a long way to come in a storm." Mom eyed me, a look on her face I didn't recognize.

"He came to see me. I guess it wasn't snowing so bad when he left." I had no clue what the weather was in Erie. I didn't wait for a response. I knew I was grody, covered in barf, smeared makeup and tears, and snow melted into my hair. I shivered as the snow trickled down my scalp.

I went to my room and wrapped my comforter around me. I sat on the floor where Kelli-Anne and I had laughed an hour ago. Omigod, I would have to call her and apologize. She left in such a hurry, I felt awful about it. We'd had fun today. It had been good to laugh, dance, and talk with a friend. Especially about Henry. The thought of him gave me an even emptier feeling in my heart. I'd chased him away, and now I'd chased away Jasper.

"Emelia?" My name followed a quiet knock on my slightly open door.

"What *now*, Alexis?" I could hear the irritation in my voice. I wasn't in the mood for her on top of everything else.

"Can I come in? Andrea is home and I wanted to talk privately."

I laughed. "Like I get any privacy in *my* room?"

She twirled the ends of her long, brown hair. "Look, I just wanted to say..." She hesitated, stepped inside, and closed my door behind her. "Your room has crappy privacy. The walls are too thin or something." She sat next to me on the floor and handed me a cup of something steamy. "I made some hot cocoa to warm you up."

"Why? Did you spit in it? Lace it with salt?" I didn't take the mug. I didn't want anything from her.

"Eh, even if I did, holding the mug in your hands will warm you up." She gave me her crooked smile.

I took it and the warmth between my hands felt wonderful. "So, you came in to tell me my walls are too thin?" Despite my resistance to her cocoa I took a sip. The warmth of the heavenly liquid soothed my frozen body and soul.

"No." She fiddled with the fringe on my blanket. "I came in to say I'm sorry. I didn't know Jasper would get so mad." Alexis inhaled a slow, deep breath. "I was just goofing around."

Alexis hadn't seen Jasper's temper before so I couldn't fault her for the blow-up. She didn't know how I shook inside when I knew I'd done something to upset him enough to break up with me. I'd never told her about the times he'd broken up with me because Phillip answered the phone when he'd called and wouldn't tell him where I was if I wasn't home. It was Phillip's thing. He didn't want someone to stalk us and kill us. He'd read in the newspaper about a girl that happened to once. Although, he really should know Jasper's voice by now. And she didn't know about the times Phillip had words with Jasper over the long distance phone calls I'd made to him. I'd rung up a tidy sum. Jasper had broken up with me that time too. I had to call him and repeatedly apologize. Each time I'd called, he'd hung up on me. I called from a pay phone, and it cost me all the coins I had in my purse. "It's okay, Alexis. You didn't know. He's not very good at taking a joke though, so maybe don't do that again?"

"Sure." She looked at me. "I really am sorry."

We didn't say anything for a few minutes, just embraced the silence while I processed the events of the day. I ran it over and over in my mind and tried to see where I could have prevented the problem. It always came back to me sitting by the phone until I'd heard from Jasper. Now he was mad and we never got to enjoy the day together. I was embarrassed Alexis had heard any or all of our fight.

"How much did you hear?" I dared break the silence first.

"Umm..." She tilted her head to let her long bangs fall out of her eyes. "Pretty much all of it."

I sighed. "Alexis, you have got to stop doing that."

"I know. I learned my lesson this time. Although..."

I sat quietly and waited for her to finish.

"If I hadn't been listening, you and Jasper might have been doing the nasty right now and Mom and Phillip might have caught you."

"That is so gross. And a terrible excuse for eavesdropping." I took a sip of cocoa. "Look, I don't do it to you so don't do it to me, okay?"

"Okay. But Emelia, the way he talked to you was totally bogus. *I* was scared and he wasn't even yelling at me. I thought he might hit you or something."

"No. Jasper would never do that." *Would he?*

"Well, I promise I won't give you away again. Sisters should stick together, right?"

The light bulb finally went off in her brain! Hallelujah. "Yes. We should."

She held up her hand for a high five. "Sisters before misters." I almost spit out my cocoa. "What?" She shrugged her shoulders as though she'd spoken a common fact. "Guys are lame."

We laughed together for the first time since hitting puberty. Thinking back, it seemed to be when the conflict had started.

"Alexis, I gotta ask. Why are you always so nasty to me?"

"I'm not nasty to you." She crossed her arms.

Oops. Too soon? "Alexis, c'mon. If we're being real here, I have a right to know what I did to make you hate me."

"I don't hate you."

"It sure feels like it most of the time."

"I didn't mean to make it seem that way. Maybe I get a *little* mad you don't hang out with me anymore. Like, ever since you started high school. You were too busy with your friends, and Jasper, so I felt like you didn't like me anymore."

"First off, I don't hang out with friends. You can see why after today, right?"

She nodded. "Yeah, but you would hang out on the porch with Henry almost every day after school when you weren't with Jasper. You let Andrea hang out with you, but not me."

"Why would you think that? We didn't care who sat on the porch with us."

She shrugged. "I just felt left out. Nobody listened when I talked or tried to show you something, so I left mad and didn't hang out there anymore."

"I'm sorry we made you feel that way, and I'm sure if Henry were here, he'd say the same thing. We honestly didn't mean to make you feel that way. We thought you didn't like hanging out with us."

"Okay. I'm sorry about all that stuff between us. I missed you." She sounded as though she choked on the words and struggled to let them out.

"Me too. And sorry about the spit in the cocoa remark. It was nice of you to make it for me."

"Why? I really did spit in it." She laughed.

"Gross!" I shoved the mug into her hands. "I'm so close to kicking your butt right now."

"Psych! I didn't spit in it." She laughed and downed the cocoa. "But, I can't promise the same for the cup I took to Andrea.

We laughed, and omigod how I hoped she was kidding.

When we finished our cocoa and brushed our teeth, I changed into my flannel pajamas and crawled into bed early. Muffin meowed as she jumped up on the bed with me

"I don't understand Jasper's moodiness lately." I pulled Muffin next to me and stroked her silky, black fur. "Just a month ago he picked me up and we went bowling and had pizza. He laughed and joked with me all night. He even loaded the jukebox with quarters and told me to pick whatever songs I wanted. We had so much fun, and it wasn't that long ago. He used to take me to dinner once in a while too. Or we'd go play Putt Putt and see a movie afterwards. He never does that anymore." A blast of memories and emotions rushed through me in seconds.

Muffin purred and rubbed her wet nose against my hand. "He used to be so happy and fun around me when we first started dating. Now I never know what I'll do to set him off and into a bad mood." Muffin meowed, as if we were having a two-way conversation. "I mean, he got my number from the personnel files and called *me*. Pursued *me*. Now he rarely calls me. So I make plans with someone else, he shows up unannounced, and gets mad at *me*." Muffin meowed her agreement.

I met Jasper the summer I'd worked selling cutlery for a local sales outfit. The job and pay sucked, but meeting Jasper had been nice. He flirted with me the first day I'd started the job. There were little winks, when the boss wasn't looking, after I did a good job on my phone pitch. Then he'd massage my shoulders while I was on the phone to customers and say "*good job, Emelia.*" He seemed to take an interest in me right away. His attention escalated until one day when he called me out of the blue. We talked and he invited me to a movie. I never game him my number.

"I don't get men, Muffin." She rubbed her head against my chin and purred. "Maybe it's just *me* that brings out the worst in him. Maybe I make Jasper miserable." Muffin hissed almost on cue at the mention of Jasper's name. I scratched behind her ears and she resumed purring.

"Those times when he's good to me make it worth putting up with the bad moods. When he's good to me, it's like all the bad memories become insignificant and go away." Muffin yawned, closed her eyes, and drifted to sleep.

So did I.

14

Wake Up Call

After church Sunday, my sisters and I had a board game marathon in Andrea and Alexis' room. It started to snow again, and we left church early when the big, fluffy flakes wouldn't let up. The roads weren't plowed and were very slippery. Phillip handled it like a champ, turning into the fishtails, back and forth up the snowy hills we went. My mom's knuckles are permanently imprinted into the dashboard.

An *Eagles* song sounded out of the boom-box. "Turn it up, Andrea." I sang along to emphasize the importance of turning the volume up louder than my voice. "I love this song. It's one of my jams." Any *Eagles* song off the *Long Run* album was my jam.

Alexis shook her head and rolled the dice to a six which landed her in jail. "I'm always in jail." She huffed and moved her iron to join me in jail.

"Me too. It's safer than going around Andrea's boulevard." Andrea had the blue and green properties locked up with three houses on each one.

"Mwah haw haw." Andrea rubbed her hands together. "You can't avoid me forever. Now, I want two more houses." She handed me the money, as I was the banker, and I handed over her new acquisitions.

"I'm not even paying the fine to get out of jail. I can sit here for three turns." I rolled doubles. "No way." I slapped my hand to my forehead and fell back into the bean bag chair. "I give up."

"You're coming my way now." Andrea rubbed her hands together again with the most maniacal grin I'd ever seen on her chubby little face. "You have to roll again."

I rolled another double, boxcars.

Alexis laughed at me.

"You're next girlie, and I see you have a small stack of ones so you're toast."

She grinned and pulled out a stack of five-hundreds from under the board. "I can deal, but you're in deep shit now. If you need a loan," she fanned the money in front of my face, "you know I want your railroads."

"Not the railroads." I pulled them back possessively. My last roll landed me on Pacific Avenue. "Of course I couldn't go to jail again." I moved my thimble to the least of the expensive properties on Andrea's monopoly.

"Pay up." She held out her hand and I gave her everything I had. "I don't have anything else."

Andrea waved her money in front of me. "I can help."

I snorted. "Hardly. I'm up the creek without a paddle now."

"Emelia." Phillip popped his head in through the door. "You have a phone call."

I sprang to my feet. "Saved by the bell." I handed over all my property to Andrea. "Good luck Alexis."

"Hey! I would have bought those from you." Alexis frowned.

"Sorry, I gotta run. You two work it out."

Jasper hadn't called since I saw him yesterday and he'd left in a huff. I brushed past Phillip to get to the phone. Jasper must not be mad anymore. When he'd left I hadn't expected to hear from him for days. "Hey Jasp." My run downstairs made my voice sound breathy.

"Emelia, it's Kelli-Anne. How are you?"

If I'd been under an X-ray machine at that moment, the world would have seen my heart visibly drop to my stomach. "I'm good."

"Sorry I'm not Jasper." Her voice was almost too quiet to hear.

"I'm glad to hear from you. You caught me off guard. I thought Jasper called to talk, after yesterday and all."

"Did it get bad after I left?"

"It was bad before you left. And I'm sorry about that." I was so freaking embarrassed. It seemed like every memory I had of Kelli-Anne being in the room with Jasper was a bad one. "But yeah, it didn't end well." I choked back a sob I didn't know I'd held back. "He left after he told me he didn't know what he wanted anymore."

"Aw Emelia. Do you want me to come over? I'll bring ice cream, potato chips, all the good junk food for a broken heart." She spoke in her Sunday School teacher voice. I'd helped her a couple times with her Sunday School class. She was a natural with the little kids. It was her sweet tone of voice and kind heart.

"It's okay. I'm grateful for the offer but the weather is too bad to go anywhere." I peeked out the kitchen curtains to see the damage so far. Mom and Phillip's cars were nothing more than mounds of white fluff. "It's really bad."

"My brother can give me a ride. He's got the Bronco and driving in the snow doesn't bother him."

"Hmm. I don't want to put anybody out. We can talk on the phone for a few." Until my mom demanded I get off because she expected a phone call, or I'd been on it too long. I wish I had my own phone in my room like Kelli-Anne did.

"It's no problem really."

"Stay inside and be warm."

She sighed. "I worry about you, Emelia."

"Me? Why do you worry about me?"

"I don't know. It's just..." She sighed again. "Don't get mad at me for saying this, okay?"

"Sure. I won't." I could never be mad at her. She was the sweetest person I knew. "You can tell me."

"Jasper scares me. Like, *really* scares me."

I laughed to hide what I really felt. Nervous. "Why would he scare you? He was mad at me because I did something stupid." I shrugged. "I do that a lot I guess."

"You totally don't. Not with me. Not in school. And you seem... different when he's around. Like yesterday, we were having fun and being silly. We were *just* laughing. But when Jasper came in the room, you were different. You changed. Everything about you changed. The way you stood, and even your voice. Emelia, I've never known you to take crap like that. Ever. Remember when you dated my brother in middle school?"

"Yeah. That was so long ago, I'd forgotten. But, I still don't know what you're getting at?"

"You never took crap from him, excuse my French." Kelli-Anne often said that. She rarely swore and when she did it wasn't *that* bad. "One time you were at our house and he told you not to cut your hair because he didn't like short hair, and you remember what you said?"

"Yeah. I threw it right back at him. *It's my hair; you don't have to wear it. I'll do what I want.*"

Kelli-Anne laughed. "Yep. And you cut it like Dorothy Hamill. It looked good on you but Matthew didn't like it. He was ticked you went and did that."

"Yeah, too bad for him." I laughed. My dad had always given me crap for something. I'd developed an attitude towards guys who told me what to do. "I dumped him because he made fun of me too."

"See? That's my Emelia. The one with spunk. You don't have that with Jasper."

"Well, Jasper doesn't tell me what to do. Or how to wear my hair."

"Doesn't he? Maybe not in so many words but he shows his disapproval in other ways."

"Like how?" I started to feel a bit defensive.

"Like getting mad and breaking up with you when you go to a party with friends. Or that temper of his whenever I'm around. It scares me. My dad told me if I ever date someone with a temper to run the other way." She paused. "Or how about when you don't answer his phone calls?"

"That was my fault. I knew he was going to call and I should have waited by the phone. Or at least had Alexis listen for it while I was in the shower."

"I doubt Alexis would have done that, but seriously Em? Can't you see it's not your fault? So you needed a shower. Big deal. He could have called later."

"I think he did. I can't remember. It's all a blur now and I don't want to think about it. I just need to grow up."

"Grow up?" Kelli-Anne huffed. I pulled the phone away from my ear. "Did Jasper tell you that?"

I didn't want to answer her question because it would give her fuel to add to her Jasper bonfire.

Kelli-Anne sighed, which told me I'd given her the answer anyways. "I love you, Emelia. I miss you and I say a prayer for you every night. You're the best friend I've ever had. But gee, you're not even 19 yet. You've got plenty of time to grow up. You have to enjoy life too."

"I do."

"Okay. So, how enjoyable was life after I left yesterday?"

Ouch. My stomach knotted. "It wasn't too bad." I crossed my fingers at the lie.

"No? Saying he's not sure what he wants anymore sounds bad to me. But whatever you do Emelia, I love you and I'm here for you. Just," she paused. I heard a loud whoosh of air as she sighed. "Be you. You're great. Don't change for anyone or let anyone define you."

"Now who's got spunk?" I laughed.

"Learned it from the best." She made a smacking sound, like she'd sent me an air kiss. "Listen, if you change your mind about hanging out, call me. Oh, and something else. The necklace."

That dumb thing again. I'd hoped she'd take it and I'd never hear mention of it again. "What about it?"

"I was looking through some of my dad's old college textbooks. He took Latin and I was trying to decipher the small words etched on the top."

"Yeah, the gypsy woman told me it meant the cycle ends where it begins, or something like that. I already tried it and the only thing that happened was it reflected some light from the window."

"That's all she told you?"

"Yes."

"Well, it says more. Did she tell you what the writing on the back meant?"

I hadn't noticed any other writing. Truthfully, I hadn't examined it at all. I'd shoved it into my pocket the day the gypsy woman gave it to me. Henry had looked at it, but not closely. "No, she only told me I could go back once."

"It doesn't say that, but I believe what you're telling me. Emelia, it says 'under a full moon, where angels spoon, thrice speak your heart, from your world depart'. What do you think it means?"

"How weird. I haven't the slightest. A lot of craziness, I suppose."

"I don't really buy into this hocus pocus, but you've gotta admit, it's fun to imagine you could really time travel. Anyways, there weren't any photographs of it in my dad's book, but I'll check the library tomorrow when they open. I have the day free and I can bring it to you after I finish my research."

"I work til six, but I don't really need it back. You can keep it. You seemed to really like it." And it kinda creeped me out, but Kelli-Anne didn't seem bothered by it.

"It'll be dark by six o'clock. And tomorrow there's a full moon," she said in a sing-song voice.

"I thought you didn't believe in this stuff."

"I don't, but like I said, it's fun to imagine time traveling." She chuckled. "And what else do we have to do?"

"Time travel is for science fiction books. And Dr. Who." I didn't have any hopes that it would work.

"But can you imagine if people could travel through time the way they drive anywhere else? Just hop into a time transporter of some sort and dial where you want to go, and instantaneously, you're there. As easy as driving a car."

"People would probably be crashing into each other trying to get to the first Christmas, or the signing of the Declaration of Independence."

"Forget that. I'd go back to the fifties. Malt shops, poodle skirts, saddle shoes, and bobbie socks. And all the dreamy hunks." Kelli-Anne sighed.

"You're thinking of Grease, and I doubt it was like that."

"I know. But I can dream."

"Sorry. I don't mean to sound grumpy. I didn't sleep too well last night. I'm tired. I actually would love to write a time travel novel. Two best friends travel back to the fifties and blow all the sock-hoppers away with their Thriller dance moves."

Kelli-Anne squealed. "Yes! I would read that book. Which makes me think, how has the writing been going? You getting anywhere on your *love* story?" She laughed.

Yeah, the notebook I tossed behind my dresser. I'll never pick it up again. I didn't dare put the words in my heart onto paper ever again. I wrote those words for me, to keep my writing sharp, not for people to read. The words were rough, and I wouldn't hand them in to a teacher for a writing project without going through and making a lot of changes. Anyways, it was a mushy story I used to practice my descriptive writing skills. And dialogue. "Nope. Haven't even picked up a pen." Not since I'd jotted down a list of possible places to look for Henry when I called directory assistance. That'd been a total bust.

"Ah, too bad. You really should keep at it. Your poetry is dark and deep. I like it."

"I'll write you a dark poem since it doesn't look like I'll be going anywhere today." I pulled back the curtain again and the snowflakes only seemed to have mutated into jumbo cotton balls falling from the sky.

"My offer still stands, ya know. Matthew will give me a ride over and we can hang out."

"Don't bother. Stay inside where it's warm. This snow isn't letting up at all. My sisters may have a snow day tomorrow."

"Ugh! My brothers are driving me crazy! They keep playing with their new Atari system they got for Christmas. Blip, blip blip. It's what I hear all day long."

I laughed. "Sorry I can't help you out."

"It's fine. I'll see you tomorrow after work, okay?"

"Sounds like a plan."

15

When In Rome

Kelli-Anne stopped by right after I got home from work. I hadn't changed out of my Fly Buyz uniform yet. I'd made a sandwich for dinner thinking I'd have time to change, but I'd taken time to talk to Andrea about her day off from school while I munched it. Alexis had hidden in her room all day and watched TV on the tiny, portable camper television. It picked up one station on a good day with its tiny antenna and today wasn't so good. Andrea told me how bored she was and would rather have been in school.

"Nobody answered their phones, so I had nobody to talk to all day."

"You had me." Phillip came in from outside where he'd shoveled snow out of the driveway. He'd parked in the street after he picked me up from work so he could get the snow shoveled out for Mom when she got home from work. It was handy having Phillip home, now that he was retired, to do things like drive me to work and shovel snow. I would've had to walk or hope to catch the city bus at the right time to get to work without Phillip around.

"You were reading your newspaper all day." Andrea grabbed a mop to clean up the fallen snow from Phillip's boots and coat. He took off his hat and shook it, which made Andrea sigh heavily, but she grabbed the mop once more.

"I was only doing the crossword puzzle. I could have used some help with the hard clues."

Phillip was a big fat liar. He did so many crossword puzzles over the last year, I'm pretty sure the puzzle makers called him for answers.

"Next time." Andrea winked at me and left me alone with Phillip and my peanut butter sandwich.

"Kelli-Anne is right behind me. Her brother pulled up as I finished the driveway."

"Oh, she is?" I went to the back door but didn't see her. I didn't even see Phillip's footprints and he'd come in only a few moments ago. "Did she fall into a snow bank?"

Phillip chuckled and stroked the snow from his neck length white beard. "I should hope not."

Kelli-Anne's face popped into the door window. She laughed and pointed at me. "Got ya!"

"Brat." She'd been ducked down below the window, which wasn't such a task for her, being only 5 foot nothing. I could never have gotten away with something like that. My dad used to call me daddy long legs, and people at school called me spider legs. My sisters always laughed at my too-short pants and called them floods. Ya know, for when the high waters come? What the heck anyways? Being five foot nine and three quarters sucked. The search to find pants that weren't 'floods' sucked more. But one day as it poured, my sisters called from downtown and asked me to borrow Mom's car to give them a ride home. I told them I couldn't go out because I didn't want to get caught in a flood. My flood pants were in the wash. I hung up and left them to walk. They came in the door about an hour later. *Good one*, they laughed.

I opened the door and looked behind Kelli-Anne. "Any more surprises? Is Matthew coming in?"

She shook her head. "No. He's gotta run some errand a few blocks over. He has to pick up something from a friend and will be back in an hour."

Yeah, I knew what he was picking up. Matthew wasn't the nice little boy I knew when I dated him. The preacher's kid gone rogue had found a way to come out from the shadows of his big brother, and make a name for himself. I never mentioned it to Kelli-Anne because it would have broken her heart. Of all the siblings, those two were the closest. She looked up to him. I couldn't take that away from her.

After I let Kelli-Anne in, I took her coat and tossed it in the dryer for a few minutes. "It'll be warm and dry for when you leave."

"Thanks." She hugged her arms around herself. "It sure is nasty cold."

"You know, you didn't have to bring it all the way over here today. I couldn't care less, but you're sweet to do it. What'd you find at the library? Anything?"

She followed me to my room, where I locked the door behind us and put on my *REO Speedwagon* album. "I didn't at first. I flipped through books on history and ancient artifacts. I guess I didn't know where else to start. I looked at books on gypsies and psychics. Even witchcraft."

"Kelli-Anne, if this thing is related to any of that, I'm out." Horror movies freaked me out, especially Poltergeist. I made the mistake of seeing that one at the drive-in with Alexis. Mom grounded Alexis when she found out, and since I was too old to be grounded, she took away my car privileges.

"I knew you'd say that, but it's better to know for sure, right?"

"I guess so."

"I wanted to rule it out, mostly." She took it out of her macramé purse and laid it on my dresser. "I figured I could bless it with holy oil if it was some creepy cursed object, like you thought. But, it wasn't listed in any of those books."

"So, it was a bust? Sorry you wasted your day." I sighed and picked up the pendant. It didn't seem so extraordinary and I probably wasted more time on it than I should have.

"You didn't let me finish." She took a slow, deep breath. "I got the idea to look in books about the Roman Empire, since they spoke most of the Latin when this thing might have been made."

"Do you think it's old?" I held it in my hand and remembered how Henry had held it in his. It connected me to him in some way, and it didn't seem as creepy. I was glad Kelli-Anne hadn't kept it. I squinted my eyes and looked more closely at the writing. "Maybe this is Latin for Made in China."

"Oh, Emelia." Kelli-Anne laughed. "Always the cynic. No, it was made near the end of The Roman Empire. About the time when it was under Christian rule. Before 300 AD, Rome had killed almost all the Christians. But by 306, Rome became a Christian empire again."

"Get out." I involuntarily gasped at her news. "No way did I get my hands on some ancient artifact." My blood ran cold as a terrible thought took root in my mind. "Do you think fortune teller woman stole it from a museum and left it with me while she's on the lamb? Do you think she'll come back for it?"

Kelli-Anne grinned and tilted her head. "You really do need to write books. Seriously, that imagination of yours." She chuckled. "No, there were many made. It was a common item religious people carried with them when they journeyed out of Rome. Some kind of reminder of where they came from for when they got where they were going. A reminder to travel back someday."

"Ahhh. I get it."

"Get what?"

"Well, the gypsy told me it would take me back in time. To a crossroads. The Romans carried it as a travel reminder. That's where she got the story." I sighed relief. "It's not really a time portal, but a reminder."

"It makes sense. So, do you still want to give it to me?" She dangled it in front of me.

I remembered how Henry placed it gently in my palm that day on my porch. How he'd pulled away his hand and grazed my fingertips. I remembered the connection I felt that day, and until now had denied. "I'll keep it." She dropped it into my outstretched hand.

"I thought you might. Now you know it's just a nice token from a long ago era and not a cursed object."

"Okay. We can stop calling it that now."

"What? Cursed object?" She laughed.

"Yes." A horn blared outside from the street. "Must be Matthew is back. That hour went fast."

"I don't think it's been an hour, but I'd better get going." She gave me a hug. "Call me okay? We'll do lunch when the snow melts."

"See ya in May then? " We both laughed, but knew a wish for melted snow before May would be pure luck.

I walked downstairs with her and got her coat from the dryer.

"Ah. This was a great idea." She pulled on her jacket and wrapped the hood tight around her neck. She barely turned the doorknob when the wind gusted in and blew the door back against the wall. "Sorry. I didn't mean to do that."

"It's not your fault. It's this crazy weather." I looked heavenward. "The clouds from that direction," I pointed over the treetops by the brick street, "are so dark and ominous." I shivered. "Tell Matthew thanks for bringing you over."

"Okay. Should I send him your *love* too?" She laughed and rushed out the door to dodge a snow ball.

"Gag me!" I shouted after her as she ran to the car.

She waved and drove off with Matthew. I was halfway up the stairs to give this time traveling gem one more try, only out of curiosity and to ease my mind, when the phone rang. I stopped when Phillip called my name.

"Emelia. It's for you. It's Jasper."

I hesitated, turned, and took one step down the stairs. One step closer to another conversation with Jasper. More like another confrontation. Maybe he decided he wanted to work things out. Maybe he'd forgiven me. Maybe we could get back on track. But which track was that? The one where I walked on eggshells all the time? Or maybe the one where he humiliated me in front of my friend? Kelli-Anne's words came back to me. I wasn't the same spunky girl I'd been before Jasper.

"Yeah, too bad for him. Tell him I'm busy and he can call later."

Ooh, Jasper was going to be so pissed at me.

16

Timelines

The pendant laid on my bed looking like any ordinary object. From what Kelli-Anne found in her research, it was more than a Gala Days tchotchke. It had a practical purpose to the Christian travelers, a reminder of where they came from and really nothing more.

I rubbed the etching on the pendant, touched the worn engraving. The words were almost erased, like time had erased Henry.

I never realized how much I'd taken his friendship for granted. He'd always been around, and I guess I didn't think that would ever change. But time changed and so had we.

I missed the way Henry would wave at me as he wheeled his bike onto my sidewalk, that goofy grin on his face. He was always upbeat and easy going. Always smiled. I didn't think he'd go off to college and never come back. I didn't know he wouldn't have a reason to come back. I just thought as time passed, he'd always be around.

But people aren't always there, are they? I should have known better. My dad left us. My mom struggled to work two full-time jobs and one part-time job as she raised my sisters and me. I don't think we made it any easier for her being teenagers, but she was rarely home. She had to do it all if she wanted to keep us together. Dad didn't pay child support either. I was with my mom the day she went to the social services office. The clerk treated her like some sort of scum off the streets. My mom begged her for help. *Can't you do anything? Can't you make him pay the child support?* The woman shook her head. *There's nothing I can do for you. Sorry. Next?*

Next? Like Mom was a random number in line with no back story.

My mom had cried. Like, really cried. I never saw her cry before that day in my entire life. She was always strong and told us to stop our whining if we fell and got hurt or didn't get our way. Yes, this strong woman cried on the fifth floor of city hall and received no sympathy from social services. I'd slipped my hand in hers as we exited the building, but she pulled away. *We'll find another way,* she'd said. She was once again composed and stood taller. I loved and hated that about her. I admired her strength because it got us through some pretty bad times in life. But I also hated it because she wouldn't allow me to comfort her. It hurt me to see my strong mother cry in front of the heartless, uncaring civil servants. I had nothing to offer her but my hand, and she'd rejected it. Like she always rejected me.

And I'd rejected Henry. My best friend.

As I remembered how Mom had rejected me, I knew how I must have made Henry feel that day.

I put my hands on my heart, as if that would stop the ache I caused it.

The cycle ends where it begins. I wondered what it meant. What cycle and where did it begin? The cycle of hurting Henry, maybe? It happened at graduation. So do I end the cycle by going to where it began? I knew it was the last time I was with Henry alone. And it was where I wanted to go.

If the travelers who left Rome carried these as a reminder to travel back home someday, then maybe I was a traveler who needed to go back home. Home to when Henry was a part of my life and not lost to me.

Maybe he didn't want to be found. I hadn't thought of it before. Maybe he didn't want me in his life, so he'd gone to a school where I wouldn't know where to find him. Maybe it's why he didn't tell me about his change of plans. But if I went back to the right time, he wouldn't have those feelings about me yet. I could change it. I could find Henry and make things right. So, maybe in my now, I'd know where he was and we'd still be friends. And I could talk to him about all the things going on with Jasper and he'd know what to say to make it better. But of course, the things that happened with Jasper hadn't happened yet.

I confused myself. Enough.

Would I go back and run into myself? Or would I be inside myself from the past?

Maybe I should circumvent running into me. But would I always have to hide from me?

This timeline shit wasn't this hard for Dr. Who.

Should I go back to before the park bench?

I called Kelli-Anne, she'd know. I looked at my watch. It had been almost an hour since she left with Matthew. She should be home by now, even in this weather. She only lived five minutes away.

"Emelia, I believe with time travel, you go to a different time-line. A different reality you create when you go back. For example, if you go back to that moment when Henry was going to kiss you, and you let him kiss you, you create like a fork in the road. Imagine a straight line. And you're traveling on that straight line until you come to a fork in the road. You make a decision to go left or go right. The path you're on is one of those two."

"Huh?"

"I know. If I were there, I could draw you a picture and explain it better. Just imagine there is one straight road and it goes from here to California. There are no other roads off that road. Now imagine you stop along the road, and you take a turn towards the desert where there was no road before. But you're creating a road. That road hasn't been determined yet. It's new and unexplored. The old road is still there, but you're not on that one anymore. You're creating a new one. Make sense?"

"Actually, that does make sense now. Thanks."

"Hey, if you do take the other road, the me from that timeline won't know any of this. So, don't freak me out and say anything."

I laughed. "You say that like it's gonna work. I'm just speculating here."

"I doubt it will do anything. But if it does, no word to past me. I wonder if maybe you do believe somewhere in your heart it might work, or you wouldn't be asking me about it."

"I guess I just kind of hope."

"And hope is made of faith. So just maybe we'll be talking about your adventure tomorrow."

"Tomorrow?"

"Yes. If my sci-fi knowledge is on point, you'll be back as though no time passed. What may take months for you, will be nothing in this timeline."

"But..."

"Yes?"

"But what if I don't want to come back here. What if I like it there and want to stay?"

"I don't know if that's an option. I'm not sure. Maybe you stay on the same path, but you have to come back to this reality or you disappear from here. What of your mom? Your sisters? They'd be worried and you'd end up on a milk carton. No, I'm pretty sure you'd come back to our time one way or another. Maybe changed.

Maybe with this reality changed. Oh, Emelia. This is crazy talk. Just, well, let me know how it goes tomorrow, okay?"

"Sure. Thanks Kelli-Anne. And if I don't come back, well, you know."

"Yeah, I know. Back at ya."

I went to my room and locked the door. I held the pendant and long chain in my hands. I recited the words Kelli-Anne told me. "Under a full moon, where angels spoon, thrice speak your heart, from your world depart."

I heard obnoxious and incessant banging on the front door.

I repeated the words and held the pendant close to my heart. More insistently I spoke the words again.

The knocking got louder and I heard Phillip holler at whoever was at the door. Probably another vacuum cleaner salesman. They were so persistent and obnoxious.

"Under a full moon." I looked out my window at the bright moon's reflected beams on the newly fallen snow. "Where angels spoon, thrice speak your heart, from your world depart." I hadn't spoken my heart three times yet.

"Emelia! Emelia! I want to talk to you!"

Jasper? Had he driven here that fast to see me in this snowstorm? Omigod. He sounded so mad. I didn't want to see him, didn't want to be here right now until he calmed down. Kelli-Anne had been right about his temper. I never noticed it until she mentioned it.

"Emelia!" His voice was loud and sounded impatient.

I heard Phillip yell at Jasper. I don't think he liked the tone in Jasper's voice. Neither did I.

"I want to go back to the bench with Henry at graduation. I want go back to the bench with Henry at graduation. I want to go back to the bench with Henry at graduation."

My head spun and the light from my room faded in and out. I closed my eyes and fell back to the floor. My head hit something hard on the way. I succumbed to the warmth and peace that blanketed me.

17

The Do-Over

"Emelia? Are you okay?" A hand held my arm and eased me along as I walked.

I blinked a couple of times and rubbed my head. Why did I have a headache? Why was I walking?

"Emelia, sit." I was eased down onto a hard surface. I grabbed my head. My legs were unsteady. I might fall over if I didn't sit.

"What happened?" I tried to open my eyes, but the light was too bright. I shielded them with my hand. Why was I outside in the snow? Wait, there wasn't any snow. Sunshine warmed my face.

"You looked like you might pass out. The heat maybe. Do you feel okay? Can I get you something?" That voice again. So close to my ear. It was familiar, but muffled and faded in and out.

"No. Don't leave me alone." I didn't know what had happened to me and I didn't want to be left alone.

"Okay. I won't leave you. Do you feel like you're going to pass out?"

I didn't recognize the mumbled voice. It was like being immersed in water while someone above spoke to me from the shore of my confusion. Hey, that was pretty good.

Nausea hit me.

"Hey, you look kinda white Emelia. I'm going to get help."

I grabbed at the arm entwined in mine before he could pull away. A man. I'd at least deciphered that from his voice. Phillip? Had I fallen and hit my head on my bedroom floor? Phillip probably heard it from the kitchen below and came to help. I remember the room going black. I must have passed out.

"I need a second is all. I'm lightheaded and a little sick to my stomach."

An arm wrapped around my shoulder. "I can see if there's any ginger ale at the reception hall. It might help your stomach."

"No. I'll be fine. I just need a sec." I braced my hands on the seat beneath me.

"I have an idea." He leaned away from me. Things started to come into focus. Wait, what reception? "Here. You like my Doublemint gum. This should settle your stomach."

His face was still blurry, but I could make out dark, shaggy brown hair parted in the middle. And dark eyes. Brown. Mmm, if this was a dream, I didn't want to wake up for a while. "Thank you." The gum tasted good to my dry mouth and my stomach stopped hurting. "My friend Henry always had Doublemint gum on him."

"Emelia? What's wrong with you?"

The dreamy brown eyes, yes, I could see now they were Hershey bar brown, blinked their long eyelashes. I stared into the eyes that were right next to mine. "You high?" He asked me.

I laughed. The idea was ludicrous. Is this what high felt like?

"It's not funny, Emelia. I know you wouldn't do that or at least I *thought* you wouldn't. You were fine when we walked down the sidewalk. But you started to shake and waver from side to side, pale as my mom's kitchen linoleum. You almost toppled over and would have if I hadn't grabbed hold of your arm."

Click. Click. Click. The wheels in my brain started to turn. The pendant. The full moon. I shook my head, hit the side of it the way my dad used to hit the old TV when he tried to bring the station into focus. Did I...? Was I...?

"Emelia, I'm freaking out here." He took hold of my hand.

"Henry?"

"Omigod." His voice oozed concern, but why?

"I'm okay now." I meant that more than he knew as I hugged my arms around his neck and took in his scent. I'd never paid attention to how good he smelled. Fresh and clean, like woodsy and peppermint mixed with a hint of lemon. "You smell so good." I nuzzled against his neck.

"You really were out of it." He looked down at me. "Are you sure you didn't smoke some weed with the stoners before the ceremony?"

"Ah Henry. You're silly." I pushed at his chest and he grabbed my hands. It was like no time had passed, us being here together, goofing around like we always had. "I would never do that. I'm stupid enough without a fried brain."

"You're not stupid. You're the most brilliant writer I know." He rubbed my knuckles, and I had a sense of deja vu. "I wish you were going to college with me." His eyes hooded with a hint of something, maybe sadness or regret.

"Henry." I loved to say his name. I looked into his eyes and saw myself reflected there. He didn't see what I saw in the mirror. He saw someone I didn't recognize.

"Emelia." His voice was soft against my cheek.

I leaned my forehead against his. It seemed like a lifetime ago since I'd seen him. We had never shared the level of intimacy we shared right now. He'd fallen onto me when we goofed around on my porch that one day, but it was a playful mishap. Although, my skin had prickled with something unfamiliar. And maybe the intimacy had always been there on Henry's part and I'd never picked up on it before now. I never was good at reading people.

"Emelia," his lips whispered against mine. "There's something I've been wanting to do all day."

Henry broke into my thoughts. I remembered this moment. It was *the* moment I'd wondered about. I knew what was coming when I asked, "What's that?"

He leaned in. "This."

And this time I didn't turn away.

18

The Kiss

Henry cradled my chin in his hands and swept his free hand over my hair. He pulled me close to him. I closed my eyes as he pressed his lips against mine. It was soft, gentle, unlike Jasper's rough bearded kisses. I kissed him back with the same gentleness, almost a reverence. I cherished this kiss and wanted to stay in this moment for as long as I could. I wrapped my arm around his waist, held him, and never wanted him to be lost to me again.

I found my Henry.

Henry pulled back, looked at me, and smiled. He ran his thumb across my cheek and held it up for me to see. "I didn't think I'd have that effect on you."

A tear? I reached a hand to my cheek. I wasn't aware I'd shed tears when he kissed me. The emotion that had been building in my heart since Henry had been gone overflowed onto my cheeks. Emotions I'd never felt before, never known existed until the moment his lips touched mine.

If only I'd done this the first time around, maybe I wouldn't have lost him. I would have realized the hidden feelings in my heart for Henry. Feelings I'd never known. Or maybe I subconsciously knew they existed and didn't want to acknowledge them.

He still looked at me, his smile gone. He caressed my palm with his thumb. "You okay? I didn't upset you did I?"

"No. No." I leaned my forehead against his. "The opposite actually." I lifted my face to his and kissed his cheek.

Henry looked into my eyes for a few long moments before he spoke. "My dreams just came true, Emelia."

My heart skipped a beat or two.

"You are the best part of my life Emelia." He held my chin in his hand, stroking it with his thumb. "I want you to be the biggest part, too." His voice was gentle.

I opened my mouth to speak, but he held a finger to my lips.

"I understand you have another relationship. I can't ask you to give that up. That's up to you. But, I couldn't let this day pass like it was any other day." He leaned in closer to me. "We're adults now and moving on from high school. I had to let you know how I feel about you before..."

"Henry..."

"I need to say this before I back out. I have had these feelings for you for a while and I know it isn't right. And I have no right to act on them. You have a *boyfriend.*" He said boyfriend like a bad taste in his mouth. "I've held these feelings in to respect your relationship, but if you feel anything for me, anything at all, I need to know now." He emphasized the word *now.* "Because if you don't, I'll leave it at that and we never have to talk about this moment again."

"Shut up Henry and kiss me again." I leaned in and he didn't hesitate to kiss me. Our hands were locked in a steeple position as we kissed. His lips were so gentle, a whimper escaped my throat. He smiled against my lips and I laughed, a little nervous. I didn't want him to think I was mushy. I wanted to stay the same Emelia he always knew, goofy and helpful with his homework. Ooh, which I now knew he never really needed. "Henry, I have feelings for you. Omigod, and I didn't even know it until you kissed me." I pulled him to me by the honor chords of his graduation gown. "And don't you dare...," My throat went dry. "Don't... well, don't leave me. Promise." I held him close to me, so very close, afraid if I let go, I'd wake up in my room with a headache, no Henry, and an angry Jasper banging on my bedroom door.

"Legs, I'm not going anywhere if you don't want me to."

"Legs?"

"Yes. A nickname." He nuzzled my neck.

"Well, it ain't gonna be legs. I'm not a frog."

Henry laughed. I looked to the cobblestone path behind us to see if anyone watched us share this moment. The path was empty. Everyone had already gone to the reception hall.

"No duh." He brushed his hand through my hair, more possessive now than the first time he touched me. "You're more like a princess. Maybe that's what I'll call you."

I sighed. "Can we just stick with Emelia? Huh? It's worked so far, and really Henry, I don't want things to change between us."

He raised an eyebrow.

"Well, some things, but not all the other stuff, okay?" I elbowed him playfully, like all the other times. "Nothing all heavy and complicated. Just you and me, with a little extra in this department." I leaned in and kissed him again. I legit enjoyed kissing Henry. How had I not done this before now? How had I not realized that an awesome kisser hid behind those amazingly full lips.

He ran his finger along my jaw before he pulled away and looked at me all serious.

"Henry?"

"I know I've complicated things with Jasper."

"Oh, we broke up." I shrugged, like Jasper didn't matter. And he didn't.

"What?" His eyes widened. "When did this happen? You never said anything to me."

Oops. It happens six months from now. Crap. This time travel stuff was tricky business. "I meant, we had a fight." At this point in time, everything was fine, or so I'd thought.

"Look, I'm not making you do anything. It's up to you." He pulled away. I grabbed his arm and pulled him down when he tried to stand. "Emelia, it's okay. It wasn't fair of me to just drop this on you all at once." He sat back down.

I'd had six months to process his feelings and to think about this moment again and again. He was living it for the first time. The first time I'd handled it poorly. I hadn't realized how badly I might have hurt Henry. I'd always taken him for granted. "Henry. We've been friends for a few years. Good friends, I thought. I don't want to lose your friendship. What if this goes bad? What if..."

"What if what?" He held my wrists and rubbed my palms, calming me.

I hung my head. "What if you decide I'm not enough for you. What if all the things I do to screw up drive you away? And," I saw my tears hit the bench. Darn it. "And I lose more than a relationship. I lose my best friend."

He tilted my chin to look at him, but I kept my gaze down. "Hey. Look at me, please." I couldn't. The tears flowed and I was embarrassed. I exuded vulnerability. Like my heart leaked all my deepest secrets. He rubbed his thumbs across my cheeks and closed his hands around them. "You've always been enough for me, Princess."

I hugged him for a long time. His warmth felt like home. What I needed and wanted all along was right in front of me, but I didn't know it until I'd lost it. "We need to keep this to ourselves until I break up with Jasper. I don't want him to find out from someone else, or by finding us together."

"I think he already suspects." He looked over my shoulder.

I looked around but didn't see Jasper watching us from behind a tree or the corner of the building. I didn't see him on the cobblestone pathway with his arms crossed and that disapproving look that sent my heart to my heels. "How? Is he here?" My voice squeaked and I cleared my throat.

"Relax." He rubbed my shivering shoulders. "He's not here. I just think guys know this kind of thing about each other." Henry sighed. "Remember yesterday, when I grabbed for your wallet in your pocket?"

Oh, yeah. That seemed so long ago. Well, it was. Only here, in this timeline, it was only yesterday. "Of course. I remember." That sick feeling in my stomach was back. Jasper had taken my photo and ripped it into a zillion pieces and stashed them into his jeans' pocket. I didn't even have a chance to tape them back together again.

"I'm really sorry. I didn't know Jasper would tear the picture. I was more worried he was going to kick my butt for falling on top of you. And honestly, I liked it, being close to you, and I was going to kiss you." Henry ran his hand over his shaggy hair. "I think Jasper knew. I'm sure he was sitting in his car longer than we realized. Longer than when we heard him slam his car door. When I think what could have happened, if I *had* kissed you." He sighed. "It would have been bad timing, is all. And it could have made more trouble for you, so I threw out the picture thing without thinking. Jasper had to have seen how nervous I was when he snuck up on us, with me about on top of you. If you want, we can let Andrea paint our faces again and take another picture. Or we can take one of those five minute photos in the photo booth at the mall."

Henry was dead serious. He would do it too. "That's fine. I mean, it's not fine the picture is gone, but I have something better now." Henry raised an eyebrow. "I have you, Henry." I leaned into his warm chest and hugged him tight to me. "I have you."

He kissed the top of my head. "You've always had me, Emelia," he whispered into my hair.

No Henry, I haven't. I've only now got you back.

"Hey, why don't we go get some cake. I know how much you love cake." Henry stood and held out his hand to me. I took it and stood, about three or four inches shorter than him. "And let's try not to ogle each other in front of everyone."

"Okay, we can try dork." I kissed the tip of his nose.

"Is that the nickname *I* have to live with? After the well-thought-out nickname I came up with for you?"

"Oh yeah, like Legs took you so long to come up with."

"Okay. We'll drop the nicknames." He smiled. "At least for now." We shook on it and moved away from each other as we headed down the cobblestone path. Only our fingertips touched as we walked.

The reception seemed long, the small talk tiresome. I remembered this moment but it seemed different this time around. I wasn't sure if I should try to re-enact what I did the first time, or go with the flow. It was a deja vu reality. When I saw Kelli-Anne with her parents and brothers, my body tingled with excitement to tell her about what happened with Henry since I'd travelled back to this time. My excitement faded as I remembered the Kelli-Anne in this reality wouldn't know anything about our conversations regarding the pendant and her research. I wanted to speak with her anyway. I hadn't the first time around. I had booked it to go home and wait for Jasper to call me. This time, I couldn't care less if I talked to Jasper.

I wondered if that would change my reality when I got back to my timeline? Hmm.

"Kelli-Anne! Congratulations." I gave her a hug.

"You too. We finally made it. Wow. Wasn't it a long ceremony? Ugh." She blew her bangs out of her eyes.

"Yeah. What were there, like 400 of us?"

"During an appointment with my guidance counselor, he told me there were 500 plus. Unless some dropped out or flunked out since January."

"That's a probability. A couple girls quit and got married. Renee Sirianno married that loser from the ball bearings plant."

"Ew. The one with the pocked, red face who mumbles when he talks?" She scrunched her nose.

"That's him. I don't get it. I tend to believe she just wanted to get out of her house." I leaned in so the nosey Olsen twins didn't overhear us. "Her mom beat her a lot."

Kelli-Anne nodded like I told her something she'd suspected as well. "And Karen from our third set psychology class got married because she *had* to." I nodded. I knew what she meant. "That guy won't stick around long. He got Jessica pregnant in eleventh grade and dumped her the day after the baby was born."

"No doubt. I don't get why these girls drop out and get married. At least with a high school diploma they can get a job if they need to. What are they gonna do when the guys leave them?"

"I have no idea. So, you heading to college?"

I shook my head. "Can't afford it. I applied for a job at the bowling alley. They're looking for someone to run the snack bar. And the Fly Buyz. They're hiring a cashier." That was the job I eventually got after graduation. But at graduation, I still hadn't heard back from anyone. "You going to college?"

"Community college. I can stay at home and it will save my parents a lot of money. And I don't really need to go to an expensive school far away to get a business degree. I wish you were going too."

I sighed. I didn't want to explain it to her. It was embarrassing. "Well, someday maybe. For right now, I need to work and hopefully get a car. Maybe save some money for college."

"Did you apply for any grants?"

I shook my head. "My parents are middle class so they make too much money to qualify for anything. What degree did you say you were going for again?" I wanted the spotlight off of me.

"Business. I haven't narrowed down a field yet, but a general business degree can take me a lot of places. Emelia, if you could go to college, what degree would you get?"

I didn't even need to think about it. "Journalism."

"I should have figured. You're good at it. Your essay in eleventh grade English, the one we all had to write and read in front of the class, that was amazing. I never forgot it."

"What had I written about?" I couldn't remember. I usually hammered out those essays a study hall ahead of the class. My hand would cramp writing the words so fast, but I always got an A or A+.

"The negative effects of fashion magazines on young women's body image. That was very forward thinking and you made a lot of good points." Kelli-Anne glanced over my shoulder.

"The guys were mocking me. Jerks. Like, let's make a magazine full of choice guys and expect the average guy to live up to that image." I smacked my forehead. I remembered how the boys in the back row made kissy faces at me, flexed their muscles, and made hand motions like they had boobs. I don't know why Mr. Morris didn't say something to them. They distracted me during my presentation. But, I guess he agreed with them and not me. Misogynists. All of them. "I was lucky to get an A- on my paper."

"It was really good, Emelia. Be proud. Don't ever let what a man thinks of you change who you are. Or what you believe." She glanced over my shoulder again and smiled. I figured I'd held her up long enough and she wanted to talk to other people.

"I'll let you get back to your family." I started to turn from her.

She smiled. "Emelia, are you still dating Jasper?"

"Yeah. Why do you ask?" I turned around to see if he came to surprise me. If maybe she saw him walk in the door. What would I do if he did show up? It would be weird with Henry and Jasper both in the same room. My pulse quickened. The palms of my hands began to sweat. Jasper hadn't shown up in my timeline, but maybe here things could be different. I had no clue how time travel worked. I caught sight of Henry. He looked my way and smiled, and I remembered I didn't care if Jasper was here. Old habits sometimes creep back in when you're not thinking. I smiled back at Henry and snuck a little queen's wave his way.

"The entire time I've been talking to you, Henry Fitch has been staring at you. I think he has a crush on you."

Heat warmed my cheeks and I turned my head away from Kelli-Anne. "I haven't had cake yet. Maybe I'll go get a piece."

"Emelia." Her voice was hushed. "Does Henry have a crush on you? You two spend a lot of time together." She closed the gap between us. "I saw you too talking earlier. *Alone*." She said *alone* like she was conspiring with me on a high-level government secret about the Russians.

I'd pretend I didn't hear that last part. "I'm still dating Jasper and it doesn't matter if Henry has a crush on me or not."

"He does, doesn't he? And you know it." She semi-danced on her tippy toes and pointed at me. Kelli-Anne sounded too happy about this. Much more gleeful than I had been to see Henry again, if that was even possible. "I won't say anything, but I can see by the way he's looking at you, and how red your face is, there is something going on between you two. Dish."

I knew Kelli-Anne wouldn't say anything, but Henry and I had made a promise to each other. I could see Henry was occupied with his academic quiz bowl friends, so I motioned for Kelli-Anne to follow me to the ladies' room. After I checked all the stalls and found them empty, I told her about Henry's confession and how I had feelings for him as well. "Please don't say anything to anyone. And especially don't let on to Henry you know. We promised each other we'd keep this between us until I have the chance to break up with Jasper."

"Tsk. You know I won't say anything. Gee, I'm so happy for you two."

"Why?" I put my hand on my hip.

"You're adorable together, Emelia." She sighed, dreamy-eyed, which made things weird. "I always liked Henry. Much better than Jasper." She mumbled the last part.

"Excuse me? Did you say you like Henry better than Jasper?" I leaned in with my hand to my ear.

"I'm sorry, Emelia. But it's the truth. Jasper gives me the creeps, the way he always... oh crap, I've said too much."

"What? What did he do to give you the creeps?" I was curious. The three of us had only hung out a couple of times. Kelli-Anne usually left once Jasper showed up. And now I knew why. One time, Kelli-Anne and I had hung out and watched corny old Saturday afternoon westerns. We'd ordered cheap pizza delivery. Jasper had happened to stop by and stayed until Kelli-Anne left. He left less than five minutes later.

"Aw, Emelia." She shook her head. "Well, I caught him staring down my top a few times. And, when I went to grab a piece of pizza, he reached for the same

piece and touched my hand a little longer than felt right."
She quivered. "Then he *winked* at me. Oh, and when I
came out of the bathroom, he was there waiting. He put
his hands on each side of the door and stared at me. And
my... boobs." She shook her head in disgust.

While I absorbed what she said, she dished some
more.

"And when I went home after hanging out at your
house, I could swear it was his car I saw following me
home. Maybe he was going the same way I was. I don't
know for sure and I'm certainly not accusing him of
anything. It was just odd and gave me goosebumps."

"The blue Nova?"

"It was a blue Nova." Kelli-Anne nodded. "But it
could have been anybody and not necessarily Jasper. It
was dark and I could have been wrong. That's why I
never mentioned it. I didn't want you to ask Jasper about
it and it not be him. I'd be a troublemaker."

I looked towards the door as a couple of girls
walked in. They walked right past the stalls and went
straight to the mirrors. They plopped their purses onto
the sinks and dug out big cans of Aqua Net and wide
toothed combs. The fog of hairspray gagged us, so we
went back out into the reception hall.

"I wouldn't have thought you were a
troublemaker, but I probably would have thought the
same thing if it would have been me." I'd never known
Kelli-Anne to lie about anything. If she said she saw a
blue Nova, I don't doubt it. But was it Jasper? And why

would he have followed her home? And why did he corner her by the bathroom at my house? And did I even care what Jasper did anymore? Nope. Not one bit.

"I waited in my car and beeped the horn until my dad came outside to see what was going on. Once the porch light came on, the car took off." Kelli-Anne relaxed her shoulders. I hadn't even noticed she had tensed them while sharing her thoughts about Jasper.

Chills ran down my arms as she told me what Jasper might have done. If I heard this story the first time I lived in this timeline, I would've had a hard time believing Kelli-Anne. I would have asked Jasper about it and he'd have convinced me Kelli-Anne made it all up. But, after what I'd experienced the last few months with Jasper, I didn't doubt it in this reality.

"I'm really sorry he did that." I was amazed that after Jasper had done those things, she was still even talking to me.

"You're not mad at me, are you?" Kellie-Anne raised her brows in concern.

"Of course not." It was a fair question. "I've had some creepy feelings about Jasper myself lately. And..." I could see Henry having an animated discussion with his friends. "I've realized Jasper isn't the guy for me."

Kelli-Anne squealed. "That's so great. You and Henry?"

"Shhh."

She spoke quieter. "You and Henry?"

I smiled and nodded. "We'll see what happens."

19

Reconciliation

I needed to tell Jasper we were done as soon as possible. It wouldn't be hard. I knew he'd cheated on me. He had enough women to keep him busy. He wouldn't miss me. Maybe I didn't need to tell him. Were we ever really official? We'd dated a couple years, but I honestly couldn't remember him ever asking me to be his girlfriend. I'd assumed we were a thing. Maybe I could wait for him to call me up for a date and I'd tell him I didn't want to see him anymore.

Had I dated one guy all this time who'd never committed to me? It didn't matter, because I didn't have the same feelings for him I had for Henry. I used to think I really loved Jasper. He'd been on my mind all the time. I looked forward to seeing him and always waited for his phone calls with anticipation. How could I have not noticed Henry? He'd always been around, at my house and by my locker. He'd always been right under my big old nose. I'd never looked at him the way I looked at him today, after he kissed me. I had been so blabby about Jasper this or Jasper that, and there was Henry the entire time. He'd offer me advice, or a shoulder to cry on when Jasper and I had a fight. Henry bought me ice cream from the ice cream truck on warm summer evenings, while we sat on my porch. Henry held the door for me when I carried a pitcher of lemonade and cookies to the porch. And there were my sisters. He'd always been so sweet to them.

Maybe that's why I'd never noticed Henry. He was nice. To everyone. I wasn't used to nice, so I guess I never thought anyone nice would be in my league. And I wouldn't be on his radar. I was used to anger and violence. I grew up in a home with two parents who acted like they'd hated each other. My dad "spanked" me and my sisters or used the rawhide strap until we had welts on our legs, backs, and rear ends. We were sent to bed early, like right after 4 o'clock dinner early, if we were too loud while he watched the Michael Douglas show. Or heaven forbid a football game. He sometimes beat us and separated us. He'd send us to different parts of the house so we couldn't play together. That's how he got his quiet house.

We were inconveniences.

I hadn't noticed Henry because he was nice. And I would be an inconvenience.

But I couldn't deny it now. When I let Henry kiss me, there were definite feelings. I hadn't felt anything like that with Jasper. If I thought I knew what love was, I knew now I'd been wrong. So wrong. There were no bad feelings about myself with Henry. There were no sexual innuendos or pressure. No guilt. If I wasn't home when he stopped by, he'd leave a little note tucked in the screen door. If my sisters were home, he'd sometimes hang out with them until I got home. And we'd become best friends. Of course I couldn't see that it could be anything more. It felt good to be with Henry and I could always be myself.

Being with Jasper was familiar. He reminded me of my dad in so many ways. It must be his temper. And how he'd yell at me or not speak to me for a week when I'd screw up. Jasper once raised his hand, but he didn't hit me. My dad made fun of how I looked and how awkward I was, tripping over my own feet. My mom told me I was ugly. Jasper told me I needed to lose10 pounds and get a tan. And he'd told me if I grew out my hair, I would look *okay*. I'd always felt dorky. His words didn't do anything to change that feeling. It was more of the same. Dad wouldn't pick me up on our weekends and holidays together. I had to beg Jasper to spend time with me. Familiar.

Henry was always there for me.

When I felt bad about something that happened at school or home, Jasper would say things like, *well my day was worse* or *you have it easy still living at home. I have bigger problems than yours to deal with. I have debt and child support. The police are threatening to arrest me if I don't pay the child support.* I remember clearly. I had $50 saved for my homecoming dress. Jasper promised he would be my date. I felt bad I had money for a frivolous dress and he didn't have any to pay his debts, so I gave him the money. When I saved $300 towards a car, he needed new tires and told me I didn't need a car. I could use my parents. So I gave him the money. All the Christmas, birthday, and babysitting money I'd saved.

Dad always took Mom's money. And he never paid child support for me and my sisters.

I was happy with the familiar until Henry kissed me. Everything I felt with Jasper now paled in comparison to what Henry made me feel. He made me feel special. He caught my tears and held them in his fist. He told me I'd made his dreams come true. And he told me I was the best part of his life.

A small sigh escaped me as I sat at my desk. I doodled while I processed all my thoughts.

"Daydreaming again, *Emelia*?" Alexis stood at the door, arms crossed as she tapped her foot.

"Hey Alexis. Wanna come in and hang out for a while? Listen to my *REO* or *Hall and Oates* album?"

"What's wrong with you? Did you fall in the shower and bump your head?" Alexis glared at me.

"No, why?" I rubbed my head, even though I hadn't bumped it.

She grumbled something I didn't understand. "Look, Mom needs some things from the store and I'm going with you." She shoved a piece of paper into my hand.

"Alexis? What's wrong?"

"Nothing's wrong." Her voice was sharp. "Why?"

I'd all but forgotten this wasn't the Alexis from my timeline. This was Alexis when we used to snap and fight with each other. I could try and win her over, but it took seeing something awful happen to me for her sisterly love bond to emerge. I'd have to go along, but my heart wasn't in it. "Fine." I stood and slammed my chair back under my desk. "Let's go."

Neither of us spoke on the way to the store and I gagged on her cigarette smoke. I cranked down my window. "Alexis, you don't want Mom to smell the smoke in her car. Roll down your window."

She did without so much as a snip.

I got what was needed on Mom's list and Alexis hit up the cigarette machine out front for a pack of something light. We were almost home when she asked me, "Why did you want me to come in and hang out with you? Are you dying?"

I couldn't help but laugh.

"Fine. Don't tell me." She crossed her legs and took a long draw on her cigarette.

"You caught me at a weak moment is all. I was daydreaming and must have confused you with my *nice* sister."

"Humph. Jerk."

Her voice didn't carry the same snark as usual. "Not really." Maybe this was a good chance to make things right with my sister. Her snarkiness hadn't been the only problem in our relationship. I wasn't always as nice as I could have been. "I really thought you'd like to listen to my *Hall and Oates* album with me. You used to like them."

"I still do. But, you never let me in your room. So, I figured you must be sick or something."

I smiled. "Or something."

"What?" She tossed her butt out the window and looked to me with wide eyes.

"I'm fine. Just trying to be a nicer sister now that I'm older."

"Well, I don't know how I feel about that. It's... creepy. You being nice to me. I'm not used to it."

The same dilemma I found myself in with Jasper. We *did* have the same dad, after all. "I should always have been nice. Ya know, with Dad and all, I guess I didn't have the best example."

She stared straight ahead. I assumed she reflected on our conversation. She didn't say anything until I pulled into the driveway. "We could listen to it now if you want."

"I want."

20

Sayonara

Just like the old days, before Henry went away and I couldn't find him, before I used the gypsy woman's pendant, I sat on my front porch with a book by my favorite author, Judy Blume. Henry rode up my sidewalk on his bike. I hadn't talked to him since graduation day. I'd wanted to be by his side and hold his hand during the reception. But as we discussed, we kept secret whatever this was between us until I had a chance to tell Jasper.

Which I hadn't.

Not that I hadn't tried. He was never in his office. The office secretary, Shelly, kept telling me he was out on appointments or out for lunch, or whatever other lame excuse he told her to tell me.

Yep, I'd found my moxie since Kelli-Anne had set me right. Since when did I let anyone dictate my life?

Since Jasper. But not anymore.

I was so close, so tempted to give Shelly the message for Jasper. *Sayonara sucker. I am moving on.*

She was always so snarky when I called. I really wanted to leave it on her to tell him.

"He *does* work, you know," Shelly had told me yesterday and the day before when I called. "Shouldn't *you* be working too?"

I hadn't started my job at Fly Buyz yet. Not in this reality anyways. "I just graduated two days ago."

"Oh, that's right. I always forget. You're still a *teenager*." She sounded like it was some kind of disease.

"Yep. It'll take me a few years to get as old as you." I couldn't help myself. She burned me. "Listen, can you just give Jasper this message?" The bomb dropped now. It'd be done and I could be with Henry without guilt.

"I don't know. We older girls have a way of losing things." Shelly was about 23 or 24, according to what Jasper had told me.

"Tell him I called and I don't, I mean to say, I can't..."

"Hold, please." She put me on hold for more than two minutes before I hung up. I had better things to do with my time than play games with Jasper's snarky secretary.

"Hey Henry." My voice sounded calm, but my heart pounded at the sight of him approaching on his bike. I'd missed him.

"Hey Legs." He skidded to a stop in front of the porch, where I sat in the warm sunshine.

"Yeah, I really think we need a different name." I remembered how Jasper played the ZZTop song *Legs,* and how my dad called me daddy long legs. "How about Babe." I smiled and flipped my hair.

Henry jumped off his bike and walked to where I sat on the porch steps. He placed his arms on each side of me and looked behind us before he kissed me on the lips. "I like the sound of that, Babe." He kissed me again, gentle. He swept his lips over my lips, rubbed his nose against my nose. I wrapped my arms around his neck and held him against me.

"What are you up to?" I whispered against his ear.

"Cruisin' around. I thought I'd stop and see what you were doing."

"Chillin." I held my book so he could see the cover.

"Is that a lovey-dovey book?" He laughed and kissed my forehead. "I'm teasing. I love that you read. Nobody in my house reads, except the ingredients on food labels." He ran his hand through his hair. "I enjoy chillin' with you and reading on your swing, talking about books. But," he placed my book on the porch next to me, "I thought today we might go to a movie. If you're free."

"I'm not doing anything. What's playing?"

"There's a new one called *E.T.* It's about an alien."

"Ooh. A scary movie." I snuggled against him.

Henry laughed. "Silly. *Swamp Thing* is still playing at the Winter Garden."

"Gag me. That one looks so cheesy. What else?"

"*Rocky 3.*"

"That one. I love Rocky movies."

"Rocky it is. The paper lists a four o'clock matinee." Henry looked at his wrist watch. "It's two now, so we have some time before we need to leave."

"I can borrow my mom's car. I don't think I want to ride on the back of your bike." I looked at the blue Schwinn laying in the grass.

"Bike? No Babe, I would never expect you to do that." He looked at me, serious as a root canal. "I have cab fare."

"No, we can walk. I like to walk." I took his hand in mine and thought how romantic it would be to hold his hand as we walked to the movies. And cuddle next to him while Rocky kicked some guy's butt. Well, maybe that part wasn't so romantic.

"We could. But you like to walk everywhere. So just this one time, let me treat you to something different. We can walk home if you want, but it's kinda hot to be walking down there in this heat."

"If that's what you'd like, it sounds fine to me."

He sat next to me on the porch and put his arm around me. Just as quick as he did, he pulled it away. "Have you told Jasper yet? About what we discussed?"

The break up. I looked up and down my street. Sometimes Jasper just showed up. I'd been pretty handsy with Henry. I hadn't thought of Jasper. "I tried calling him and he's never in. I got his snarky little office secretary, who acts like his wife or his mom. I was going to leave the message with her, but she put me on hold." I crossed my arms. "He should know I've been calling, and as far as I'm concerned, he acts like we are already broken up."

Henry shook his head. "Emelia, you dated him for two years."

"So?"

"So, you really should make things clear with him before, you know, we are seen together in public."

"We've been seen together lots of times. This isn't much different."

"We weren't seen doing this." He pulled me to him and kissed my lips like we were the only two people on the street. Like old lady Pitt didn't peek out her curtains, and Mr. Ainsley didn't weed in his garden, or the mailman didn't walk the sidewalk on the other side of the street.

Like it was just the two of us. When he pulled back he looked at me with hooded eyes. "Please tell him, so I don't get my butt kicked."

I laughed. "You won't."

"Uh hmm. Okay."

"What does that mean?" I played with the hair that fell in front of his eyes and twirled it around my finger.

"It means I don't think you understand guys. And it may look to him like you're cheating on him. Which technically..."

"I've thought about that. I don't think he ever asked me out officially. We just dated for two years. Nothing was ever declared." This conclusion was a recent one, based on what I'd experienced with Jasper in my timeline six months from now. At this point in time, when I'd first lived through it, I was still blindly devoted to Jasper.

"Emelia."

"Okay. Okay. I'll go inside and try to call him again." I flipped his wrist to look at the time. "He should be back from lunch by now." I ran a hand through Henry's tousled dark hair. It was soft to the touch. Did Henry use hair conditioner? I smiled, gave him a kiss on the cheek, and went inside.

Phillip would kill me when he got the phone bill with these long distance calls to Jasper. And I didn't want to make the calls any longer than necessary by chatting it up with Ms. Shelly Nosey-pants.

"He's, um, busy right now." Shelly's voice sounded raspy and winded.

"Well, he needs to get unbusy for one minute. It's all I need."

"Why do you keep bothering him? He's a busy man."

"I wouldn't have to keep bothering him if you gave him the phone so I could talk to him. I'd never have to call again." I was tired of her bullcrap.

"Never?"

"Nope. I just need one minute."

"Hang on, Emelia." That was the first time she'd ever used my name.

I waited at least an entire minute before Jasper picked up the phone. "Emelia. Hey, what's going on?" He sounded a little winded, too.

"Hi Jasper. Sorry to bother you at work. I don't know how else to reach you."

"That's fine. I was, um, finishing a meeting with a client." He cleared his throat. "Shelly said it sounded important though, so I rushed him out of my office so I could come to the phone. Are you okay?"

"Yes, I'm fine." I stuttered to try and say what I needed to say. I looked towards the screen door where Henry talked to Andrea and laughed about something. It was most likely childish. Guilt grabbed hold of my heart. No matter what I did, I would hurt someone. I needed to get this done. I figured the best way to do it was to rip it off like a Band-Aid. My mom always insisted it was the best way to do it. "Jasp, I'm not sure what this is between us, or where it's going, but...I can't do it anymore. So, I called to say good-bye."

I waited for some kind of reaction: questions, pleading, even laughter. I heard him take a deep breath, but he didn't say anything.

"Jasp? I guess if you don't have anything to say, I'll let you go. Um, thanks for..." What, exactly? I came up empty. He hadn't even come to my graduation. "Some good memories." There. That would cover anything I couldn't think of right now."

"Okay. Well, don't let the door hit ya in the ass on your way out of my life." And he hung up.

That was the same line he gave me in my timeline when I'd left him. He'd let me go, but he came back eventually.

Would he come back this time too? I didn't think there'd be any problem with him letting me go.

At least, I didn't *think* so.

21

The Promise

Henry and I had hung out many times before, but this time was awkward. I wasn't sure how to act around him. Should I be like a girlfriend or still treat him like my best friend? Was it okay to still be silly around him, or should I be more grown-up, like Jasper wanted me to be? And would he mind if I held his hand in public? Jasper never let me do that. He'd yank his hand away. He said it was clingy and needy. Adult couples didn't need to show affection in public.

I felt comfortable enough to ask Henry. "Hey Henry?" We'd walked from the movie theatre after seeing Rocky, which was so good. Mr. T was a real tough guy. The entire movie theater cheered as Rocky knocked his block off and Mr. T finally fell to the mat. We walked to a little diner uptown for burgers and milkshakes. Henry insisted it was his treat.

"Yeah, Babe?"

"Um, I was only kidding about that nickname. You don't have to call me that." I squirmed in my seat, as a middle-aged couple looked our way. They smiled like they were in on our little secret.

"So, back to Legs?" He tilted his head and laughed.

"Um, if you want me to throw a spit wad at you." I held my milkshake straw and rolled the wrapper between my thumb and finger. "No. You see..." I didn't want to tell him too much so he'd tease me, but I really wanted him to understand why I didn't like that name. "You see, Jasper used to play that song by *ZZTop* when he was with me..." My voice trailed off, as bad memories appeared in my head. I didn't want to think about them, now.

He placed his hand on mine, which I hadn't known trembled. "I won't call you that. You don't have to explain anything." He lifted my hand to his lips and kissed it like I was a princess. His princess. "Is that what you were going to tell me a minute ago?"

"No. I was thinking we've been friends for a while and now we're doing this, whatever it is..."

"Dating. People call it dating." Henry gently rubbed the knuckles on my hand.

"Okay. Dating. Like Jasper and I did for two years."

"No." His smile faded. "Not like that. Not like that at all, Emelia. Like on a regular basis. I call you and we go out on dates. Every Saturday night, we have a regular date night."

Ooh. I never had anything like that with Jasper and I now understood why I probably hurt Henry's feelings. "I'm sorry. I keep mentioning Jasper, and I don't mean to."

"He was a big part of your life for two years, Emelia. I understand." His eyes were warm and I knew he meant it. "I used to hear all about you and Jasper and honestly, the guy took you for granted. I won't do that. I want to spend time with you so much, you'll get sick of me and send me home."

"I doubt it." We still held hands. "Henry, is this okay?" I looked at our hands.

"Is what okay?"

"Holding hands in public. You don't mind?"

"Why would I mind? Oh, don't answer that." He closed his eyes a moment and shook his head. "Yes. I want to hold your hand. I want everyone to know you're my girl. Is that okay? Can I call you my girl? Because I don't want to date anyone else but you."

I felt my smile wrinkle my face up to my ears. "Absolutely. I don't want to see anyone else either, Henry. I only want you."

He squeezed my hands and leaned over the table to kiss my forehead. The lady at the table next to us sighed and smacked her husband on the arm. "Why don't you do that anymore?"

I heard him stammer and mumble something back to her, but she didn't seem to buy it. She still chirped at him like an angry mama bird. I couldn't help but smile.

"You're the best part of my life Emelia." He sat down, but his hand never left mine. His eyes didn't either.

"Is it okay, now that we're officially dating, if I still call you a dork and punch you in the arm when you make fun of me? Can we still hang on my porch swing reading and getting face painted by Andrea? Or is it not cool for couples to do?"

"I don't know what all couples do, Emelia, and I've only had one other girlfriend."

Nasty Nicole. She wasn't very nice to Henry and was always mean to me when I was around them. She'd cheated on him, too. And she made him spend all his money on her going to fancy restaurants and rock concerts in Buffalo. I didn't want to take away Henry's money. "Yes. I remember." I rolled my eyes. It was instinctual anytime her name came up in conversation.

He grinned. "Yeah. So, I am just making all this up as we go along. As far as I'm concerned, I don't want to change any of the things we do together. I enjoy all those things. We're just going to add to what we already do." He winked and my face warmed. I knew what he meant. It wasn't dirty, but he wanted me to think it was.

"Oh, like roller skating?" I laughed and he did too.

"Whatever my babe wants."

"I'd like to walk home and sit on my porch for a while. With you." I placed my hand against his cheek and he leaned into it, eyes closed.

It was the perfect summer evening. Not too hot, not too cold. Perfect weather for a walk. Henry held my hand and I was glad it wasn't too hot. It would have been embarrassing to hold hands if mine were sweaty. I noticed his were mostly soft, with a few calluses at the base of each finger. I rubbed his palm with my thumb as he lifted it to his lips and kissed the back of my hand.

The walk up the hill to my house, past all the Sears and Roebuck homes spattered with a few Victorians, reminded me of the walk I had after I made the phone calls to the colleges. When I'd been looking for Henry. It also reminded me of my conversation with Rosalina. She'd mentioned Henry had done homework until late at night at the sub shop to avoid home. I had never asked Henry about his home or his parents, and wondered if now would be a good time to do that. Or was it too soon? I'd never met his parents. I knew they were old, and I wondered if they were dawn of the dead old. Old people creeped me out a little bit with their crepe-like skin and sunken in eyes. I liked them well enough, but their looks creeped me out.

What did Henry do to get calluses? And for what reason did he avoid his home? I figured it was too early to ask those questions as a girlfriend, but as his friend, I was duty-bound to ask.

"Henry, I realize I don't even know where you live. And actually, I don't really know much about your family."

"Not much to know." He squeezed my hand in his and swung it back and forth to the rhythm of the crickets. "My parents are pretty old. I love them but, well, they kind of embarrass me. All the other parents are into coaching their kids' sports teams and the moms are on the PTA. My dad works at the tool plant and comes home late after drinking at the bar and spending all his paycheck." He brushed his free hand through his windblown hair. "My mom cries herself to sleep most nights, after they fight. And when he comes home drunk without his paycheck." He stopped right there on the sidewalk before the intersection and lifted my chin to look at him. "I hate my home. I love my parents, but I hate my home. That's why I started hanging out at your house. Your family is nice."

I snorted and thought about Alexis.

"Even Alexis." He kissed my nose. "When you're not home, she sits on the porch with me. When she sees you coming home she runs inside and tells me not to tell you she was out there with me."

"Why would she want it to be a secret?"

Henry shrugged. "I don't know. Maybe she thought you wouldn't want her talking to your friends."

"Naw. Andrea does it and I don't care." Maybe Alexis was hiding a little crush of her own. For Henry.

"I don't know. Maybe she didn't want you to know how nice she can be."

I laughed. "Perhaps." Knowing what I know now, that could be true.

"I like Phillip. He shares all the latest news in the paper with me and he doesn't treat me like a stupid kid."

"Because you're not, Henry. You're a smart guy."

"I guess."

"What? You were class valedictorian for goodness sake."

"I just studied hard. And I had you to help me with those essays and English papers."

I bit my tongue. Kelli-Anne had filled me in on his excellence in English and math, but I didn't want to say anything to give away his secret. We crossed the street when the light changed and walked the last block to my house at a slower pace. I wasn't sure which one of us set the new, slower pace. Maybe it was both of us. But we were quiet. The only sounds were the peepers and a cat fight.

"Henry, when do you leave for college? And which one again?" I figured this was my chance to find out where he would be so when I got back to my timeline, I could find him. I didn't know when this whole once back and forward, or whatever, would end and I needed to know so I could find him when I got home.

"August. Remember? We talked about it a few times. And I'm going to Cornell."

"Oh that's right. I get Cornell and Corning mixed up sometimes."

"I really wish you were coming with me."

"I'm not the brain in this relationship. I have to stay here and work until I get enough money to afford college. But I need a car first, I guess."

He held my hand, didn't say anything, and swung our arms slightly as we walked the rest of the way. It wasn't quite dark and nobody was home. All the lights were off inside and on the porch. The north star and the moon strained to shine in the light of dusk, competing with the setting sun. We sat on the porch swing. Henry wrapped his arm around my shoulder and pulled me close to him. "Emelia. I want you to know I would never get drunk."

"Okay. But, you're going to college. There'll be lots of drinking and you'll want to fit in."

"I won't. I won't end up like my dad. And I wanted you to know, because I was thinking about what I told you earlier, about my mom and dad, and I didn't want you to think I'd end up like my dad."

"Oh Henry, that never crossed my mind." I hugged him around the waist and snuggled my head under his chin. He returned my embrace and rubbed my arm when he kissed the top of my head. "You're not your dad."

He seemed to hold me tighter. He drew me close to him as if he thought letting go would make me disappear. "I would never hurt you, either."

"I know."

"I would never, will never, make you cry." He squeezed me and I stayed quiet. I let him mull over whatever deep thoughts went thru his mind. My sweet Henry. So opposite of Jasper. "I don't want to leave you and go to college."

That was a bomb. "Henry, you have to go. You have an opportunity to make something great of yourself. You're very smart and you'll make a wonderful veterinarian. It's what you've always wanted to do."

He sighed but didn't speak right away. "That was before I met you, Emelia. Being a vet became second to wanting to be with you once we met."

"Henry, you say the sweetest things, but I really want you to promise me you'll go to Cornell." And if he kept his promise, and I knew him to be an honest guy, I'd find him at Cornell when I got back to my timeline. But really, if I'm being honest, I didn't want to go back and risk losing moments like this. I didn't want to lose my best friend again. I'd always have Kelli-Anne, and I loved her to pieces, but Henry was a different kind of best friend. He was the kind I could kiss and snuggle with on my porch swing. "Promise me, Henry."

"But I'll miss you. We've only found each other."

"No, Henry. We found each other freshman year in our horrible science class when I could not for the life of me get my knife to cut through the poor frog's belly."

Henry laughed. Really laughed. "I am grateful for that frog. If he hadn't been such a tough skinned amphibian, I wouldn't have worked up the courage to talk to you."

"You were skilled at slicing and dicing the poor little guy."

"Ugh." He placed his hand on his forehead. "That was bad."

"I guess it was. But you handled it like a pro. You were made to be a vet. Please, don't give up your dream. Promise me. Promise me you'll go to Cornell in August and study and not worry about me. I'll write. I'll take a Greyhound out to visit you. Actually, Phillip goes out that way to visit his mom and he likes to visit his old school. I'm sure they'd drop me off to visit while they do their thing."

Henry rubbed my cheek and leaned in to kiss me. His lips were soft and warm. I didn't hesitate to return his kiss, even though I knew it was his attempt to shut me up. And to avoid my questions. The entire tropic in general. But, I liked it when Henry kissed me. I'd never been kissed so loving and tender. He made it seem like holding me and kissing me was enough. He ran his finger along my jawline, which sent quivers all the way to my toes. He stopped what he was doing to look at me. "You are amazing. You would do all that for me?"

"Of course. Why wouldn't I?"

"I didn't think you'd want a long distance boyfriend. Again."

Oh. Well, I could see where he was going with this. Jasper and I hadn't worked out and perhaps Henry feared a similar fate. "Do you think there's another guy who'll let my sister paint his face like a dog or lion, and want to sit on my porch with me?"

"It could happen. There are lots of us guys who enjoy a good face paint." He smiled at me.

"It won't. I promise to save my heart for you, Henry Fitch. Until you decide you don't want it anymore."

"Don't say that." He ran his finger along my arm. "Geesh, you're dooming us before we even know where this is going."

"I'm kidding. I'll be working as much as I can so I can save lots of money. The four years will go fast."

"It's eight years, Babe."

My heart hit my big toe. "Eight years? Oh, gee Henry."

"You change your mind?"

"Never. I just think I'll have to work 24 hours a day to make enough money to get out to college with you." I smacked my forehead.

He laughed. "You planning to come to Cornell?"

"I doubt I could afford it. But Corning maybe. I don't know. Maybe I'll never afford college."

"I promise."

"Come again?"

"I promise to go to Cornell in August and study to be something. I can't promise vet school though. I'm not sure that's what I wanna do anymore. I've been thinking about bio-engineering."

"Thank you." And those were the last words spoken for the next half hour, until we heard the loud slam of a car door and heavy footsteps on my sidewalk.

22

Hot Henry

"Hey you two. What are you up to? Star gazing?" Phillip stepped onto the front porch and removed his cowboy hat.

My heart was still in my throat when Henry answered, "Something like that. How are you tonight, sir?" Henry stood and shook Phillip's hand. Something I'd never seen Jasper do. My heart melted a little bit more for Henry and his respect for my step-dad.

"Oh, you know. Those councilmen won't listen to me." He scratched his buzzed head. "I've been telling them for two years now the light on Prendergast, by the old elementary school, isn't facing the right direction."

Oh boy. Phillip was passionate about his roads and bridges, as a retired highway man himself. Henry was in for a lengthy conversation I had heard several times already. "I'll get us some iced tea, Henry. Would you like some, Phillip?"

He shook his head and kept on with his conversation. Henry gave me a dagger-filled look as I left them alone to discuss the inappropriate light placement on Prendergast Avenue. I took my time as I removed ice from the trays and filled the glasses. There wasn't much iced tea left in the fridge. I sighed as I poured a nice glass for Henry, and water for myself. I drank it down, looked out the front window to see Phillip animatedly swing his arms, and poured myself another glass of water.

I smiled while I watched Henry smile and nod at everything Phillip said. Henry never interrupted him and only spoke to say *I agree, good point, I like the way you think.*

"Why you smiling?" Andrea snuck up behind me and looked out the window to see what had put that smile on my face. "Never mind. I see. Henry is *hot*."

"Andrea," I gasped. "Do you have a crush on Henry Fitch?"

"Well, sure. He's adorable and sweet. And hot."

Of course a 13-year old would admit to a crush on an older guy. It seemed so out of reach and impossible, who would think anything of it anyways? Kind of like my crush on Shaun Cassidy in middle school. I had his posters on my wall, and all the Teen Beat's with him on the cover. It was a girlie fantasy, much like what Andrea probably felt. At least, I didn't think she had any real intentions for him. And I suspected Alexis had a little crush as well.

"He likes you, though. And I wouldn't take him from you."

"Oh does he?" How long had she been home, anyways? Had she seen us together on the porch? "Where have you been all night?"

"We went to the county fair. You weren't here, so Mom took Alexis and me. Phillip had another one of those dumb old meetings, so we went without him."

"Oh. When did you get home?" I was curious if she'd seen Henry and me cuddle and kiss on the porch swing.

"Just behind Phillip. Why?"

So, I'd been inside getting the iced tea when she got home. "No reason. The house was dark and I didn't know where everybody went."

"Yeah, well that's where. Mom saw Phillip and Henry on the porch talking and thought it'd be a nice night to sit out and have ice cream. So she and Alexis went back out to the grocery store."

"That does sound good." My tummy growled. "So, what you said about Henry..."

"Being hot?" Her pupils dilated.

"Um, that's weird coming from you. No. The part about him liking me."

"Yeah? You didn't know? Everyone else can see it. But all you see is *Jasssperrr.*"

My gut swirled at his name. I hoped Henry wouldn't hear it through the open window. "Shh." I took her arm and moved her away from the window. "Jasper and I broke up."

She stood on her toes and squealed. "Omigod! It's about time! I mean, sorry, if he dumped you." She covered her mouth in feigned regret. She'd never hidden her feelings about Jasper. All it took was one shush from Jasper when she sang along with her Diana Ross album, while we sat in the living room, to turn her against him. She balled her hands into little fists, her face as red as her Hoppity Hop, and I hurried her into the kitchen before Jasper noticed her. She could be a wrathful little child. Mostly, as even-tempered as a saint, but get her riled, and she would hold nothing back.

"I dumped him, actually."

"Really? Wow, just the other day you were going on about how much you *looooved* him and wanted to marry him someday."

"I did not."

"Yeah you did. Don't you remember when you were getting your graduation gown ready and you went on about someday it would be a wedding gown and a tiara, instead of a cap and graduation gown?"

I had done that. But it was six months ago in another world. Literally. "I was a gushy moron."

Andrea laughed. "Well, as long as *you* said it, I don't have to."

"Ha-ha. I've learned a few things since that day."

"Like what?"

"Like Jasper can be a real jerk."

"No duh. Like I knew that."

"Yes. You're smart." I patted her shoulder. "And Henry told me he likes me, so we're going to see where it goes."

"What does that mean? I mean, I knew Henry likes you. He's always coming over and waits for you, even when you don't come home early."

He had reasons other than me. His home life. But I wasn't going to share that information with Andrea. "It means that we are going to date and see if we get along."

"Phtt. You two always get along." She hugged me around the waist so hard, I nearly lost my balance. "I'm really happy. I like Henry. And I *know* he loves you."

"Whoa. Nobody said anything about love."

She leaned back to look at me. "If you could love jerky Jasper, I know you'll love hot Henry."

She may have a point. "What makes you so sure about that?"

She placed a forefinger on each temple. "Because I can see the future." She laughed.

Well, little sister may be on to something.

23

Unworthy

Andrea carried Henry's iced tea and I made her promise not to say anything. "Be cool sis, okay?"

"What? I'm not a total dweeb."

Let's hope not. Phillip still entertained Henry with tales of highway chaos. He looked to me, his eyes pleaded for help. "Here's your tea, Henry." Andrea handed it to him and I couldn't help notice her mouth something I couldn't make out. He gave her a discreet thumbs up. I started to think they had a secret and I was going to find out by the end of the night.

"Thanks Andrea." He took a long, slow sip. He gazed at me over his glass. It was probably time I rescued him from Phillip's pontification before I gained and lost a boyfriend all in the same day.

"Hey Phillip, Mom is in the kitchen looking for you." I gave him a knowing nod. "She's scooping ice cream."

"Ho-ho. My honey bunny knows I love ice cream." He looked to Henry. "Nice talking with you, Henry. Do you need a ride home later?"

"No sir, thank you. I have my bike."

"Oh, don't get me started on bike riding in the dark. You know, I had a little boy come out between two cars riding his bike. All I saw were the big whites of his eyes before I hit him." Phillip frowned and shook his head at the memory.

I smacked my forehead. Poor Phillip. He rehashed the events of this tragedy a lot, as though it were some sort of confession or penance for his part in the accident. He was a Methodist, but Mom had converted him from Catholicism. Perhaps the art of confession was still ingrained in him. The little boy was okay; the bike had taken the brunt of the hit. But his eyes haunted Phillip still, and it had happened years before he met my mom. "Phillip, do you think you could tell Mom I'd like a scoop of vanilla. Henry, would you like some ice cream?" I nodded in his direction so he'd take the cue to say yes and we could send Phillip on his way. I loved him, but his filibusters were sometimes the bulk of any conversation.

"Yes sir, I would like some. Two scoops please."

"Okay. I'll let her know."

"I'll bring it out to you." Andrea followed Phillip inside. She turned only to give us a thumbs up. I owed her for her play of interference.

I plopped down on the swing next to Henry. I sloshed some of my water onto the swing cushion. "Oh, I'm sorry. Here." I took off my sweater to sop it up, but Henry stopped my hands before I could do it.

"It's fine." He pulled a red bandana out of his back pocket like a magician and sopped up the dampness.

"You carry a bandana in your pocket?" I covered my mouth to hide my smile.

"So? It's more cool than a handkerchief."

I laughed at the image of him with a hanky neatly folded, peeking out of the pocket of his black t-shirt.

"You are incorrigible, Emelia." He tossed the bandana to the ground, placed his arms around me and pulled me in to his warm body. He looked over the top of my head, "There are faces peeking at us through the window, ya know."

"Yeah, we're not alone anymore. We can be grateful we had *some* time alone."

He whispered against my ear, "Not enough. Not enough time for me to kiss you as much as I want."

A sigh escaped me, but I didn't think he heard it. I had a feeling I'd be doing it a lot with Henry. Had I ever sighed when Jasper kissed me? Maybe in the beginning, but I had no first time memory of it.

"You can kiss me, Henry. I don't mind." I teased him. I didn't think he'd want to kiss me in front of my family. My sisters. And what would Phillip think?

To my surprise, he placed his lips against mine and tugged my bottom lip. "I was hoping you'd say that," he whispered. His kisses were chaste and exhilarating at the same time. I don't think he meant to have that effect on me. I pulled back and turned my face towards the full moon above the trees across the street. "Isn't it beautiful?"

He looked to where I did. "Yes, it is." He wrapped his arms around me and held me to his side. "Did I do something wrong, Emelia?"

Perceptive Henry. But I couldn't share what was on my heart. That I was unworthy of him.

"No, Henry." I leaned into him. "You've done everything right."

Henry left shortly before eleven. He didn't want his parents to worry about him.

"You can use our phone to call them," I offered.

"That wouldn't work. We don't have a phone."

That would explain why I'd never gotten a phone call from Henry, or why he'd never asked for my phone number. He never needed it anyways. He just rode by my house on his bike and stopped to visit.

"Do you want Phillip to drive you home? I know he wouldn't mind. He would probably feel a lot better about it than having you ride home in the dark."

"Eh, I do it all the time. Don't worry about me." He kissed my nose and worked down to my top lip. When Henry kissed me, I forgot everything else. "I better book." He pulled away from me.

I held onto him a few more seconds and kissed him again. "Thank you for the movie and dinner. I had a nice time."

Henry gave my waist a squeeze and pressed his lips to mine again. "I'll stop by tomorrow, if you want. The county fair is still going on tomorrow, if you'd like to go with me," he whispered against my lips.

The last time I went to any kind of fair had been the Gala Days where I met the gypsy fortune teller. That time it hadn't been with Henry, but with Kelli-Anne. I instinctively pressed my hand against the pocket of my cut-off jean shorts and felt the pendant. "That sounds like fun."

"I won't be over before noon, so you get some sleep."

"I'll ask Mom if I can borrow the car. It's a long walk to the fair, and a cab would be too expensive."

Henry nodded. "Good idea. I better run." And after one more quick kiss, he hopped on his Schwinn and peddled home.

24

Baseball Bats And Panic Attacks

I laid awake for a long time. So much happened in a short time. Henry had been direct with how he felt and what he wanted. And when I asked him about his family, he didn't hesitate to explain about his dad and mom. What must it be like to live in a home like his? I never met Jasper's parents either. Which was fine, but when I asked him about them, he changed the subject. He never took me to meet them during the two years I dated him. Did I want to meet Henry's parents? Would he want me to meet them? In my timeline, they'd moved away right after Henry graduated. I wondered if Henry already lived alone.

I slept past nine the next morning. I took a hurried shower before I tore through my closet for something to wear to the fair. I chose my Jordache jeans and white eyelet t-shirt with flutter sleeves. It was my favorite and I had it since middle school. I couldn't part with it. It was soft from being worn so much, which made it my most comfortable top.

Excited to see Henry, I hopped down the stairs two at a time and went into the kitchen to make some toast. My sisters were up, bleary-eyed. They'd stayed up late with Henry and me. They both beamed when I walked into the room. I guess the hand-holding and stolen kisses didn't get past them last night.

I ignored their big grins. They probably already had a plan to razz me a little bit about Henry. It didn't matter how old I was or who I dated, they always had something immature to say.

But they didn't say anything. They ate their toast, talked about their friends, and some girl they knew that got pregnant and dropped out of school. I listened, but didn't add anything to the conversation. My thoughts drifted to the fair, Henry, and how much longer I had in this time-line. I wondered if I'd be able to stay here forever.

"Is Henry coming over again today?" Andrea asked before she took the last bite of her toast.

"Yeah, he's coming over this afternoon. We're going to the fair."

"It was okay." Alexis took a drink from her juice glass. "Nothing new or different. But I like to get a couple bites of a candy apple every year." Alexis was barely a size 6. It bugged me because I could never fit into any of her cute clothes.

"I'm going to ask Mom if I can use her car so Henry doesn't have to pay for another cab. You can ride along if you want to go again today."

"What's this about me?" Mom breezed into the kitchen, a potted plant in her hands, hair tucked neatly under a bandana. She set the pot on top of some old newspapers on the counter.

"Henry wants to take me to the county fair today. Would it be okay to use the car? He paid for a cab to the movies yesterday and I don't want him to pay for a cab again today." I held my breath and waited for her to answer. Maybe I should have asked Phillip for his car instead.

"Well, that would be expensive. I'm not using it today for anything." She dug up her plant and placed it into another pot she had off to the side. "I'm replanting flowers and working in my garden. If I need anything, I can use Phillip's car." She stopped what she was doing and gave me her crooked smile, something she rarely did. "So, you and Henry, huh?"

My sisters giggled. Now I knew why they'd been quiet. They would let Mom tease me about my new relationship.

"We're dating, I guess."

"You guess?" She stood with her hands on her hips. "Does Jasper know?"

"I called and told him. He didn't really care and hung up on me."

"Rude. That guy never had any manners. Reminds me of your father." She dug more aggressively into her bag of potting soil. And that was all Mom had to say before she tossed me the keys from her purse and left the kitchen.

I gave Alexis and Andrea a stern look. "You two couldn't wait to tell her, could you?"

"No duh! Wait until you run into Phillip!" Alexis laughed and ran from the room.

I leaned my head into my hands. Andrea lightly touched my arm. "It's okay, Emelia. We all like Henry, and when we talked about it last night while watching TV..."

"You had a family pow-wow about it already? Geesh!"

"Don't have a cow. It was pretty exciting seeing you two finally admit your feelings for each other. We were beginning to wonder if it would ever happen."

"How come I never noticed?"

"Jasper." Andrea frowned.

"I guess so." I shrugged. "I was really in love with him."

Andrea spoke quietly, "No. Jasper." She pointed out the kitchen window to the blue Nova parked out front. Jasper strutted up the sidewalk to my house, tight jeans, a light blue, diamond print shirt unbuttoned almost to his naval.

My heart fluttered. He was sexy all dressed up, his hair recently cut, and his car sparkled like it had just been washed and waxed. It didn't hide that hideous bungie cord attached to the hood though.

Andrea placed her hand on my arm. "Emelia, don't fall for him again."

"I won't." I cleared the frog from my throat.

"I see that look in your eyes. And you know how he can talk you into anything." She looked at Jasper as he came up the sidewalk and gave him her middle finger. "I hate him. If he ruins things with you and Henry, I'll... I'll... I don't know what I'll do, but when I figure it out, it'll be something big."

I understood her concern. Despite what I knew about Jasper, I couldn't help the attraction. He walked with a swagger of confidence that made my heart leap. My stomach fluttered with a kaleidoscope of butterflies.

"Remember the bad too, Emelia." Andrea stood to go to the door. "Remember the gut retching and crying. Remember the raccoon eyes from ruined mascara. Henry doesn't ever make you feel that way. And remember how he told you to lose weight and your hair was too short. Henry likes *you*, Emelia. *You*. Just the way you are."

She went to the door before Jasper could ring the doorbell. I glanced at the kitchen clock. Henry wouldn't arrive for another couple hours. I had plenty of time to deal with Jasper and send him away. Andrea was right. I didn't want Jasper. Hadn't I come back in time to find Henry after I realized what a jerk Jasper was? The tingles he gave me were nothing compared to the warmth and acceptance I had with Henry.

"Emelia. It's *Jaaaspeeer,*" Andrea's tone was out of character, a bit nasty. "He wants you to come out onto the porch." She looked at me from behind the door and shook her head. I had to deal with him once and for all. A phone break-up hadn't been the best way to handle things with him.

I went to the door and the smell of Polo aftershave hit me. My knees quivered. Omigod, it smelled so good on him. Jasper's jeans were tight. Too tight. I looked away to hide the warmth which was most likely visible on my cheeks. I was embarrassed for him.

"What do you want, Jasper? I told you, this isn't working out. I don't want to see you anymore." I kept my voice firm, and even a little bit louder than I usually spoke to him.

Jasper pulled out a fistful of flowers from behind his back, as well as a box of drug store chocolates. "I want to talk to you." He leaned in towards me and tried to give me a kiss. I turned my head away. Ironic. It's exactly what I'd done to Henry. "I got you something."

I took them and laid them on the bench inside the doorway. "What is it you want to talk about?" I crossed my arms.

"You're so cute when you're mad." He placed a hand on my arm. "Come for a ride with me and we'll talk."

"We can talk here." I stood my ground, even though he smelled so good. And looked so good too. My knees buckled, but he caught me with both hands.

"I know you still love me. Whatever you think I did, we can work it out."

"It wasn't anything you did."

"Was it Shelly? Because we're just friends. Really good friends. I know she gives you a hard time on the phone, but she's protective like that. Ya know, the gargoyle to the boss." He chuckled and ran a hand through his blond hair. My gaze followed the motion.

I cleared my throat and pulled away from him. "It wasn't Shelly. Well, she is a ditz, but that's not the issue." I looked down at my sneakers. "I don't want to see you anymore. You're never around anyways, and omigod you didn't even come to my graduation. I haven't even heard from you since before graduation. It's time we're done."

He stood closer to me and spoke in my ear. "Is that what this is about? I'm not giving you enough attention?" His tone was harsh. "Get in the car and I'll take you somewhere now. Wherever you want to go."

I didn't like where this conversation was headed. He stood close enough to me that his chest hairs tickled my neck.

"No. I'm not going anywhere with you." I spoke a little too loud. If my sisters were around, I hope they heard me.

"Shh. This is between me and you. Let's go somewhere and talk."

"Talk here. Whatever you have to say, I'm listening."

His face contorted in a way I'd never seen. It turned dark and emotionless as he raised his hand towards my face. He pulled it away and ran it through his hair. His expression was only dark for a millisecond before it became pleasant again. His big toothy smile was back in place. His brilliant blue eyes sparkled. "Why are you doing this to me? Did you ever really love me?" He sat on the porch step and put his head in his hands.

I looked heavenward and summoned a deep breath. Jasper looked at me with tears at the brims of his eyes ready to fall onto his cheeks. Guilt washed over me like high tide on the beach. I hadn't wanted to hurt him. I sat next to him. The pang of guilt in my gut only grew when he placed his hand on my knee. "You're so beautiful." He gazed into my eyes. "And you're a wonderful person." He took a deep breath. "I never imagined me with anyone else."

"Oh, Jasper. Can't you see it's not working? I need a secure relationship. Someone I can count on." I tried to explain.

His look pleaded with me and my heart once again softened.

"It's just... well, you've made a mistake. We belong together. I promise, I will change." He got on bended knee and took my hand. "I don't know if I can live without you."

"You can. You've pretty much done it all this time." My breathing quickened. He might not leave. I looked at my watch and it was almost noon. I wanted him gone before Henry came to pick me up. If he saw Jasper, I don't know if he'd leave or get mad at Jasper or maybe even at me.

"I can't." He wiped tears from his cheeks, and for the first time I knew they were phony crocodile tears. "I'll kill myself. I will." The ultimate attempt at blackmail. Jasper had just sunk to a new low, even for him. "I just can't live knowing you aren't in my life." His tone sounded more desperate. His usual tricks were not working on me.

"I'm so sure." I looked into his eyes. Jasper thought too highly of himself. This was a ploy. And I knew it.

"I mean it, Emelia. I will do whatever it takes to make you see I can change." Still on bended knee, he rubbed my hand. I pulled it away in disgust.

"Stop it, Jasper. You are upset, but you don't mean anything you are saying. You will be fine. You're a busy man, remember? You have so much to do, you barely have time to talk to me on the phone."

"I'll make the time. I'll be better, I promise."

I shook my head and looked over at the vines that grew on the trellis of the porch. They strangled the delicate lattice work and covered its own beauty, much like I was strangled by Jasper's neediness right now.

"I think about you all the time."

"Not even."

"I do. I was so busy trying to make money so we could be together and I neglected to call you. I'm doing all of this for us, sweetie. I love you."

Bomb. Drop. The three little words he'd never uttered to me. The words I had dreamed all my life of hearing someone say to me.

"No one will ever love you like I do. You're making a big mistake ending something so beautiful. I want you to be happy and I want to be the one to make you happy." He made a promise he had no intention to keep.

His eyes were so sincere. My head hurt and my stomach twisted. "I need to go inside. I can't think right now. Please, go."

He looked at me, something like hope in his eyes and a smile on his face. "Please, come with me. Or let me sit with you and we can talk. Like we did when we first met. Remember those nights sitting at Jimmy Jacks coffee shop? The hours we spent laughing and sharing our dreams and hopes?" Jasper's voice was hypnotic, so smooth and enticing, even after everything he put me through.

"I do. Yes. Those were nice times." I rubbed at the pounding in my temples.

"It can be like that again." I knew this was another empty promise.

"Jasp..."

"I know you still love me." He sounded certain that I did. "Nobody will love you the way I do. Nobody."

"I need you to leave. You're confusing me." The hot sting of tears forced their way to my eyes. Why did he choose now to tell me he loved me? I wanted to hear that from him in the worst way for almost two years.

"I don't want to leave without you." He reached for my hands, but I pulled them behind my back.

"You heard her. She asked you to leave." A low, quiet voice from the sidewalk drew my attention away from Jasper and straight to Henry.

I whispered Henry's name. I couldn't bear to look into his eyes. I couldn't bear to cause him pain. What if he thought I'd invited Jasper to my house? What if he thought we were reconciling?

"Fitch. Always coming around at the worst times." Jasper stood, wiped his eyes, and returned to his confident composure.

"I'd say it was the perfect time, dude." Henry walked past him onto the porch and stood between me and Jasper. "If a girl says leave, she means leave."

Jasper grunted. "Mind your own business, Fitch. Hop on that little bike of yours and peddle home. Leave a man to take care of his business."

"Stop it! Jasper, that's *so* mean." I looked at him and saw him for the manipulative monster he was. "You really need to leave right now!" My knees trembled, along with my hands.

Henry placed a hand on my arm. "Emelia, breathe babe."

I did. I took in a long breath and let it out slowly. I guess I'd yelled at Jasper louder than I realized. Phillip came to the screen door and asked what was going on. Phillip furrowed his brow, the way he did when he wanted to say something but thought better of it. He looked at me, raised his cowboy hat, and scratched his stubble. "Emelia? You okay?"

I shook and the words wouldn't come. My breaths came in rapid successions and made me lightheaded. Andrea came to the door beside Phillip and took in the scene. "Phillip, Jasper is upsetting Emelia. Right Emelia?"

I nodded. Now bent over, I tried to breathe. Jasper was a monster, an evil monster that only wanted me when he couldn't have me. And when he did have me, he treated me like crap.

"Get her a paper bag. She's hyperventilating." Phillip spoke to Andrea, opened the screen door, and walked to my side. "Try to breathe slow, Emelia. Long and slow breaths." He gently rubbed my back in a soothing motion. He looked at Henry and Jasper. "Which one of you is responsible for this?"

"I just got here, sir. I don't know what's going on." Henry moved back from me, a confused or hurt expression on his face. I wasn't sure which.

I managed to point at Jasper. That prompted Phillip to send Jasper on his way. He straightened to his full height of six foot five and looked down at Jasper. "You need to leave young man."

Jasper stood indignantly and puffed out his hairy chest. He really needed to learn to button his shirt. It wasn't the seventies anymore. And he didn't intimidate people as much as he thought he did. "Only if Emelia wants me to leave. We were talking and I don't know what brought this on, but I want to make sure she's okay." Jasper pointed an accusatory look in Henry's direction. "She was fine until Fitch showed up." Henry visibly sunk back a little further into the shadows of the porch.

"No." I managed between gasps.

Andrea was back. She handed Phillip a paper bag.

"Here Emelia." Phillip held the open bag against my mouth. "Try to breathe normally, okay?" Phillip continued to rub my back.

I did as he instructed. It only took a few inhales and exhales for my breathing to return to normal and the lightheadedness to subside. "It wasn't... Henry." I looked to Phillip. "It's Jasper. I need him to leave."

"No, she's not well. She doesn't know what she's saying right now." Jasper moved towards me and placed a hand on my arm. My flesh crawled under his touch and I jerked my arm away.

Phillip wouldn't have it. "You leave right now, or I'll get my baseball bat and that can show you the way to your car."

Ooh. Wrong thing to do, pissing off Phillip. He was mild-mannered and pleasant, but don't mess with any of his girls. Alexis chose this time, after Phillip's booming voice pronounced violence upon Jasper, to make an appearance. "What's happening?" She looked from Jasper, to me, and to Henry in the shadows. "Ahh." She came out on the porch and took a seat on the swing. Geesh. This wasn't a spectator sport.

"You'll regret this." Jasper's voice was low, almost dangerous. "You don't know how good you had it with me. Nobody will ever love you the way I do. Nobody." Jasper ran a finger along his exposed chest. Even now my gaze followed the movement. What kind of power did he have over me?

Andrea appeared with Phillip's baseball bat and Phillip took a couple of practice swings. He'd been a pinch hitter in the days when he played on the city baseball league. I could envision it now: Jasper's head soaring over the pine trees across the street and onto the next block. That image made me smile.

I'd never seen Jasper turkey trot so fast and it made me laugh. Finally, I could laugh again.

"You okay, Emelia?" Phillip swung the bat from side-to-side and waited for my answer.

"I am now. Thank you."

"What happened?" Alexis asked.

I looked to her and saw she sat next to Henry on the swing, who also seemed to anticipate an answer to her question.

I winked at her. "I'll tell you about it later, I promise. Right now, I need to speak to Henry." Nobody made an effort to move. "Alone, please."

Alexis groaned. Andrea lifted her to her feet and pulled her inside the house. Phillip followed and closed the door behind them.

Henry and I didn't speak for a few minutes. What could I say? It looked bad. Jasper had reached for my hand and I hoped Henry hadn't seen that. I didn't initiate it and had pulled away. I did feel guilty for the attraction I had for Jasper when he showed up at my door. Now the image turned my stomach and I gagged. Henry must wonder what we talked about and if we'd gotten back together.

Henry placed a hand on my shoulder. "You okay, Emelia?"

"I think so." I swallowed down the bile that had risen into my throat.

"Did he," he inhaled sharply. "Did he hurt you?"

I shook my head. "No. Not physically anyways." I rubbed my head, trying to ease the headache. "But, he kept saying things and confusing me."

Henry sighed and rubbed my neck. The tension lessened when he did.

"I do dumb stuff. Say dumb stuff. I shouldn't have broken up with Jasper on the phone. I hurt him." I looked at Henry. "I don't want to hurt you, too."

He took my hands in his. "You won't."

"Henry, it must have looked awful. Jasper and me like that. I promise, I didn't want him here."

He rubbed my knuckles and kissed my forehead. "It's okay. You don't have to talk about it."

"When I was dating Jasper, I let you kiss me. That was cheating. Why would you trust me, ever?"

He didn't say anything. He made circles on the back of my hand with his fingers. "I don't know, Emelia. I really don't know what to think right now. I'm still letting it all sink in. I heard him giving you reasons why you should give him another chance. And from what I saw, you were asking him to leave. I guess that's enough for me."

I fell against his chest and let the pent up tears run down my cheeks. The emotional toll on my body finally released. It made me shaky. He pulled me into him. We didn't speak for what seemed like a long time. He gave me exactly what I needed. His hugs.

Henry tilted my face towards him and brushed his lips gently against mine. The warmth of his kisses and the strength in his arms gave me the assurance I was home. When we pulled apart, I looked into his soothing brown eyes. "Henry, I know I made the right decision choosing you."

He nodded and put his hand over mine. "I'm glad you did." He nuzzled against my neck. "Are you still up to going to the fair? You scared me when you weren't breathing right."

"I feel fine. A little weak from all the emotional drama. The fair should get my mind off it."

25

The Fair And Old Acquaintances

Henry and I arrived at the fair early enough to see the animals, my favorite part of the fair. My least favorite part was to see them in cages, with blue ribbon winners marked sold to local meat markets.

I tried not to think about that. It might convince me to be a vegetarian.

The pigs were so cute with their curly Q tails and the way they snorted in their sleep. The bunnies were a close second. So many fluffy ones.

I smelled the curly fries from across the midway. My stomach growled at the delicious aroma.

"You know I forgot about this, but it's concert night." Henry entwined his arm in mine as we walked.

"Do you know who's playing?" I looked around for a handbill that might be tacked onto an electric pole or barn post. "Oh, here. It says *Alabama*. Aren't they a little big league for our small county fair?" *Alabama* had been on the charts the last couple years. Whenever *Love in the First Degree* or *Feels So Right* came on the radio, I turned it up and released my inner country chick. I was still a closet disco fan but since everyone declared "*Disco Sucks!*" I kept it to myself.

"They might have booked them before they got popular. Maybe the fair committee was able to afford them at the time. I don't think a little place could book them at today's rate."

"Let's do all the attractions on the outskirts of the fairgrounds first and move inward. That way, we'll be able to hear them play. It won't be the same as seeing them, but I'm okay with it."

Henry nodded. "Good idea. Where would you like to go first? Are you hungry?"

Just as I said *no,* my stomach let out a major growl.

Henry laughed. "What would you like?" When he looked at me, his eyes reflected the carnival lights all around the midway. They made his brown eyes sparkle and flash with color.

"The curly fries smelled good." I caught a glimmer of the jewelry booth and my legs carried me there. "I'll be right here when you get back."

"I can wait for you." Henry followed me around the jewelry cases. In one, there was a locket etched with butterflies.

"I'd like to see that one, please?" The older gypsy man nodded and removed it from its case. I reached in my pocket for my wallet and found the pendant in the back pocket of my jeans. My heart raced a little. I hadn't even thought about having it on me. I patted it with reassurance and reached to my other back pocket for my wallet. I had some money and the necklace was only five dollars. The locket contained a photo of a woman from the 18th century on one side and a man dressed in western garb on the other. I wondered what their story was? Did they travel cross country in a covered wagon to settle a homestead in the wild frontier? Did they love each other and spend their days raising a family? Did they grow old together?

It's a stock photo, Emelia. My imagination dreamed up stories all the time. I couldn't help myself. "I'll take it," I told the older gentleman behind the counter. He nodded and took a polishing cloth to wipe it down for me. I reached into my wallet for a five-dollar bill.

Henry rested his hand on mine. "I've got it." He handed the man five dollars and change.

I smiled at Henry and he leaned down to kiss my forehead. "It's all on me tonight, Babe." He swept my hair aside and dangled the locket around my neck. He fastened the clasp and kissed my nape. My heart melted a little bit more for Henry Fitch.

He took my hand in his as we walked the midway. I looked at all the attractions and tried to decide which one to go on first. The line to the bumper cars was the longest, but also my favorite ride. It was right next door to the jewelry booth where Henry had bought my locket. "I'll save us a place in line while you grab some fries."

"You sure? The line is backed up for at least, hmm, I'd guess at least thirty minutes."

"Yeah. Go ahead. There's nobody at the curly fries concession. By time you get back and we chow down the fries, we'll be ready to ride."

Henry laughed and jogged over to the food concessions. I leaned from one side to another. I counted the people in line ahead of us. I got to 25 when someone bumped against me. I turned to see the man from the jewelry counter polishing his case.

"I'm sorry. I didn't mean to bump you."

"It's no problem, my dear." The voice was not a man, but a woman. She turned to look at me, the unmistakably familiar face of the gypsy woman from the Gala Days. Her cerulean eyes bored into mine. "I see you used the time twister to go back to the crossroads, yes?"

My heart pounded against my ribs. Breathing became labored, like one of the blue ribbon pigs sat on my chest. The gypsy woman took my hand. "It is okay, dear. I am not a ghost."

"You? How?" I smacked the side of my head in an attempt to bring my mind into focus. "I'm not well. I've lost my mind." I moved to a ruff hewn bench beside the jewelry booth and fell onto the seat. I took slow breaths. Phillip wasn't here with a paper bag this time.

The cerulean eyed gypsy sat next to me. "It is well, my dear. You are not losing your mind." She didn't laugh. Not a chuckle, a snicker, or even a smirk.

"You... you are the fortune teller. Why? How are you here?" My brain buzzed with activity, processing the scene in front of me.

"I am a fortune teller, my dear. I also help my husband with the jewelry when business is slow for me."

"Oh." Of course. Like that explained everything. I'll just be on my way now. Pip-pip and cheerio. Omigod, the heat must have fried my brain. I could see Henry in line for fries. What was the hold up? He was only the second one in a short line. He noticed me watching him and shrugged. When he lifted his hand to his mouth, mimicked taking a drink, I nodded. Good. Henry was where he was supposed to be. I had only imagined the gypsy woman.

To add to my annoyance, I turned to see the gypsy woman and shrieked.

"Do not be afraid, dear one. I am only here to guide you back. It has been the required amount of time. Once back, remember. Only once, but always a way home." She patted the top of my hand. It was cool, even in this torrid heat. "I am here to help you home."

I looked at Henry. Panic. That's what happened in my body right now. I wanted to run and stay at the same time. My hands shook and my knees trembled. "But, what if I don't want to go back?"

She nodded. "You see. You didn't listen to me." She wagged her crooked finger at me. "The choice, it was a gift. To save you heartache. But you went with your heart, not listening to your head." She tapped her kerchief clad head.

"I don't understand. My head never said anything."

"It did, but you could not hear it over the beating of your own heart. Now, you have come back to the crossroads you sought. You have seen what could have been. But you know what is."

I nodded. "Yes. I do. But," I looked at Henry again. He'd moved to first in line at the counter. "I want more time with him. I can't find him in my timeline. He's... " Tears welled in my eyes as my voice cracked. "He's gone."

"All is not lost to us. Sometimes, things are just... misplaced."

"What was all this for? Why did I have to see this?"

"You wanted to see it."

Grr. She was right. I did this to myself.

"Can't I stay here and change my past. Now that I know what the right path is?"

"No, dear. Nobody has the power to change their past, only their future."

Tears slid down my cheeks. I'd been so blind. "My head, it knew Henry cared for me. I knew I cared for him." I lowered my head, looking at the wood grain in the bench. "I denied it. I couldn't believe someone so kind and thoughtful could love... I mean, care for me."

"Sometimes, we ignore that which we believe is right in favor of what is familiar."

Yeah. My dad. Jasper. That was familiar. Henry was not like either of them, so how could he see me? And still care for me?

"He saw you all along, dear Emelia. He saw what you were blinded to by the familiar."

"How did you know what I was thinking? Oh, never mind." I waved her off. She didn't surprise me anymore. "How did you know any of this, right? It's a mystery. But since you know so much about me, how much longer do I have with Henry?"

"You have until 11:45 tonight."

"Not midnight?"

"Eh, that's so cliché. Eleven forty-five tonight and you will go back to where you left as if nothing has changed. But Emelia, something has changed. We both know." She tapped her head. "Don't forget that."

"What's changed? I'm going back to the same empty world without that sweet guy over there." I tilted my head in Henry's direction.

"You have changed."

"Emelia." Henry jogged over to me, fries and two Cokes in his hands. "Who was that lady you were talking to?"

The lady who gave me everything, and took it away? "The wife of the jewelry booth owner."

"I was worried when you were sitting here with her. You looked a little pale, and I thought you must be sick to get out of line."

I looked over to the line and noticed it had grown twice in size. "The bumper cars have lost their appeal."

He handed me the Coke. I drank down half of it, stopped to burp, and downed the rest of it.

Henry didn't laugh. "Babe, here." He handed me his Coke. "Are you sure you're okay?"

No, I'm not okay. Because in a few hours, I'm going back to a world that you're not in. "I'm not feeling up to any rides right now."

He nodded and handed me the fries. "These are good. Maybe you need to eat a little something."

"Children, there is a barn dance tonight at the horse barn. The horses have been taken to the pasture for the night and there is music for all." The gypsy woman held on to her husband's arm. Both smiled at us.

"Oh, I don't dance." Henry held up a hand in protest. "I have two left feet and bad rhythm."

"It is up to you." The old lady shrugged and gave me a wink.

Hmm. The last time I didn't listen to her things went bad. "C'mon Henry. It'll be fun." I nuzzled into his side. "Our first dance. Please?"

Henry sighed. "If you'd rather dance than ride the bumper cars... "

"I would." I looked at him with hope. "I need a little time to regroup. I'm still feeling the effects of this afternoon's drama." I placed my hand on my forehead.

Henry's hands tightened into fists. "You could be. Sure, we can dance a bit. I'll try anyways."

As we walked towards the horse barn, lit with gaudy colorful lights and covered in pink and brown streamers, *Alabama* started to play *Feels So Right.* Maybe I had made the right choice for once. I hoped it was the first in a long line of right choices.

26

The Dance

The barn had been shoveled out, thank heavens. I couldn't imagine dancing in horse plops. The smell lingered even though the open design of the barn allowed for the evening breezes to air it out. The hay bales had been left around the sides of the barn. A few wallflowers waited on them for the music to start. It wasn't crowded. I presumed not many people knew about this dance.

Henry held my hand as we walked through the barn. We checked out the sights and sounds of the barn turned dance hall. I wondered if this had been a last minute decision on someone's part. The floor was dirt, but packed firm. The streamers on the outside doorway of the barn didn't compare to the streamers on the inside. It looked like a party supply company threw up in here, but in a good way. The pink and brown streamers hung from the rafters and floated down around our heads, almost touching Henry's. Chinese lanterns placed around the barn cast a lovely light, transforming the atmosphere from a vibrant fairground to a romantic haven.

"This is interesting." Henry looked at the streamers and tugged on one. "Someone was busy doing all of this."

"I kind of like it." I leaned into him. "It's a good place to dance and relax. I needed something like this tonight." I looked up at him. "Someplace to be alone with you. No family, no theatre full of patrons, and no..." I stopped before dropping the 'J' bomb. "Drama. No drama."

Henry squeezed my hand. "There isn't any music, though."

"I can hear *Alabama*. Barely."

"We can't dance to that. We'd be the only ones."

"Oh, who cares. Nobody here knows who we are. At least, I don't see anybody I know." I scanned the barn for a familiar face.

Henry glanced around the barn too. "I guess you're right. But how can they call this a dance without music?"

As if on cue, a trio of men walked into the barn, guitar, bass, and drumsticks in hand. They walked to a corner where there was a raised platform and the guy with the drumsticks lifted a tarp off a shiny set of drums. Next to it was a steel guitar. "He must play both," I surmised out loud.

The tall man with black hair and a short beard looked at the meager gathering and sighed before he spoke. "Y'all can dance to the concert music if you'd like until we get set up here. It'll be 20 minutes or so."

I nudged Henry. "You see? It's okay."

He sighed. "Do you want to dance right now?"

"No. I don't hear anything right now. They might be playing a slow song we can't hear. We'll wait for a fast one."

He led me to a hay bale next to an open window. "I know you don't think you can dance Henry, so thank you." I squeezed his arm.

He tilted my chin to look into his hooded brown eyes. "I can't dance. But with you in my arms, I can do anything." He leaned in for a kiss and tears stung at my eyes. The reality that this would all be gone in a couple hours hit me like a baseball to the gut. "What's wrong Babe?" He ran his hand through my hair and tucked the tendrils behind my ears. He kissed my cheek and spoke softly against my lips. "It'll pass. These bad memories. It will take time, but I'm here to fill your life with good memories. And they will overshadow all the evil you've seen and felt."

I couldn't contain my tears. They fell like sheets of water on a windshield during a flash rainstorm. I kissed him with the fervor of a war bride. My life had been a war. I'd fought to keep evil at bay and hold goodness close.

I wanted to memorize every detail of his lips against mine and how amazing it was. I ran my hands through his shaggy brown hair. It was soft as cornsilk. I wanted to remember how it felt in my fingertips. "Thank you Henry." I whispered into his ear. "You are a gift, and I will never forget this night."

"Babe, we have a lifetime of nights like this ahead of us."

His words tugged at my heart. When *Alabama* started again with a fast song, Henry stood and pulled me to my feet. "Emelia, will you dance with this clumsy oaf?"

I hugged him. "Of course I will. I wouldn't want to dance with anyone else."

We moved onto the dance floor. Some teenage girls followed our lead. They swayed together and laughed to the music.

Henry gazed into my eyes and sang along with the lyrics of *Love in the First Degree*. I wasn't sure I could handle it. "I didn't know you knew this song."

"Yeah, I know a few of their songs. I mean, how can I not? They're on the radio all the time."

"You could have turned the station. You're a hard core rocker. Or that's what I thought, anyways." I winked at him.

He wrapped his arms tighter around my waist. "You thought a lot of things, Emelia. And I'm going to change the way you think about those things."

"Oh, like what kind of things?" Where was he going with this? A little panic rose inside my chest.

"Things like Jasper. Things he said to you. He was wrong about a lot of things. But one thing in particular really got to me."

I laughed, trying to veer away from the topic.

"It's not funny, girl. I'm serious." He twirled me around like nobody else was in the room.

"Why Mr. Fitch. You are a pretty good dancer."

He nuzzled my neck. "I'm good at a few things you don't know about."

I tingled at the innuendo and he looked at me with a crooked grin. "Not what you're thinking, dirty-minded girl."

I laughed. "Well, what kinds of things?"

"First back to what I started to say. About changing your negative thoughts about yourself."

"I don't have negative thoughts about myself." I protested. "Well, not all the time."

"Jasper was wrong earlier. I'm sure many other times too, but let's take this one at a time."

"About what?"

"That nobody will ever love you the way he claims he does. I could love you." He pulled me into him and held me tight. "I do love you. I always will."

I waited for him to laugh and say *Psych*, but he didn't. He held me close and we continued to dance to the song *Alabama* played. The audience cheered and I imagined them cheering about what Henry had said to me.

"I love you too, Henry. I always have." I hadn't expected to say it. But we didn't have much time before I went back to my time. I needed to say it. I needed him to hear it.

We didn't talk for a while. Our bodies swayed as one to the music long after it ended.

The trio started their rendition of *I Believe in You*, by *Don Williams*. "I've always thought this song was beautiful." I wrapped my arms around Henry's neck and stood on my toes to kiss him.

His hands were in my back pockets. It was comfortable. Normal. Something you'd expect from two eighteen year olds who'd just fallen in love on a horse barn dance floor. "You're beautiful." He whispered into my hair. "My Emelia."

27

Fade To Black

We danced to all but one song, and that was only because I had to visit the ladies room. We clung to each other like it was our purpose. I snuck a glance at my Timex while I waited in line for the ladies' room. It was five minutes to eleven. My throat tightened. I didn't want to spend any precious time away from Henry. This line moved too slow, so I skipped out and went into the men's room. A little trick I learned from my grandma years ago at my cousin's graduation. No line. And in no time I was back in Henrys arms, dancing to another song.

"Aren't you tired, Emelia?" The ends of Henry's hair were damp. It was a sexy look on him.

"I'm not tired. I don't want to miss a single dance with you."

"We'll have plenty of dances. Can't I rest for at least one song?" His eyes pleaded with me.

"No. I gave you one song while I was in the ladies' room." Er, men's room actually.

"That was less than five minutes. Just one song?"

Henry didn't know we wouldn't have plenty of songs. If the gypsy lady told the truth, and her track record had been 100 percent so far, I'd be gone in fifteen minutes. What would happen to Henry when I vanished? Would he be left alone on the dance floor? Would the Emelia from this timeline take my place and was there even another me here? Would this entire reality fade into nothingness when I left? Would Henry fade away? I wanted to tell Henry about all of this, but he'd think I was crazy. For sure. Like, I was totally out of my mind. And who could blame him? He could say it was the stress and drama of the day. Maybe he'd blow it off until he realized I was gone from his life and nowhere to be found.

"Henry, I need you to know something." I led him from the dance floor. We walked outside to where there were no lights on us. The crickets dominated the early summer evening. Alabama's music was long gone, and the rides were far enough in the distance they didn't cast any light on us.

Henry rubbed his hands up and down my arms. "You're shivering." He removed his denim over shirt and draped it on my shoulders. It smelled of him. Rugged and woodsy, mildly peppermint with tones of lemon. It was soft against my skin. My shivering had nothing to do with the cool summer breeze and everything to do with my last moments with Henry.

"Thank you, Henry." I stood on my toes and held his face in my hands. I moved my lips gently over his. They were soft and sexy. If I had to blip out of here, I wanted it to be with Henry's lips on mine.

He didn't ask why I'd dragged him outside, he simply returned my kisses. His hands stroked my middle back and rubbed upwards to my neck where he stopped and cradled it in his strong hands. Tears welled again. My heart raced in anticipation of my leap out of his arms and back to my room, where an angry Jasper pounded at my door. Maybe I could blip back a few minutes early to climb out my bedroom window and escape down the oak tree. I didn't think that would happen though.

I forced myself to pull away from Henry. I had to ask him one more time, to be sure, so I would be able to find him when I returned to my timeline. "Henry, promise me again."

He nuzzled his nose against mine and kissed my top lip. "I promise."

I swatted his shoulder.

"Hey. What's that for?" He smiled and jumper cabled my waist. I squealed and squirmed away from him.

"I need you to promise me you'll go to college. Don't stay here."

He didn't smile. His hands held my arms and his deep brown eyes searched mine for something. "Why do you want me to go? I love you, Emelia. I don't want to leave you."

Omigod Henry, and I don't want to leave you. "I love you too, Henry. More than I ever knew I could." I took his hands and looked into his eyes. The sparkle in them from a moment ago was gone. "I want you to know I will always love you, whether you are here or away at college, that won't change." I brushed his windblown hair from his eyes to see they were welled with the same tears I'd held back.

He leaned his forehead against mine. "I finally have you to love, and to hold, and now you're asking me to let you go? I can't."

"This is what's best for you. You can't get ahead if you stick around this town. You need to take the opportunity and make something of yourself. Don't waste your talent for me. I'm not worth it."

"Don't say that." His tone was firm.

I sucked in a deep breath.

"I'm sorry. I'm so sorry. I... " He ran his hand through his hair. "I'm not great at good-byes." He wrapped his arms around me and pressed his body to mine. "I'm much better at hellos." He kissed me with the passion of a hero who would give his life for me. I couldn't let Henry give up his life for me.

"Henry. You are smart and gifted. You're valedictorian of our class. That's a big deal."

He shrugged. "It's just grades, Emelia. I can go to college here and still be successful. And we can be together."

The world around me faded. Henry's grip on me wasn't solid or real anymore. I needed to know where Henry was in my timeline. If he wanted to go to our community college, I'd know where to find him. But maybe he wouldn't be there either. The gypsy fortune teller explained I couldn't change the past, only the future. My future. And this wasn't my past to change. It was the past I could have had. It was a past I could never get back or have again. The only thing I'd accomplish now was freaking Henry out. "Okay, Henry." I kissed him. "I don't want you to go either. I want you to stay with me forever." My hands on his cheeks, I kissed him and stared into his eyes, "Henry, you do what is best for you. And know that no matter what, I love you."

Henry's breath hitched. "Emelia, there's something I should tell you."

"What's that?" My voice didn't sound like my own.

"It's about college. I don't want you to carry the burden of guilt when I don't go to Cornell. You see, about college... "

"What, Henry?" His voice faded and I couldn't make out all the words. Something about not feeling guilty when he didn't go to college. "You mean *if* you don't go, don't you?"

My mouth moved, but the words were inaudible. Henry's lips moved and I heard muted sounds, like I was under water. The lights dimmed and the music faded. My head felt light, and the world I'd come to love, the world where Henry Fitch loved me, faded to black.

28

No Place Like Home

"Emelia? Emelia, wake up." A hand patted my cheek. I tried to open my eyes. They were crusted shut, like waking from a long night's sleep. "Emelia." Again a warm hand patted my cheek.

I couldn't make out the voice. It was muffled. "Henry?"

Someone grunted. "She's lost her mind. Maybe she fell and hit her head." That was not Henry's voice.

"Be quiet. Didn't I tell you to get out of here anyways?" That voice was definitely Phillip's.

I blinked open my eyes and rubbed my head. It didn't hurt too much. Phillip stood over me with a look that told me I'd given him a scare. I reached for his hand. "I'm okay, Phillip." I feigned a smile. My mind was foggy. How long had I been gone? Was it all a dream? It all seemed like a dream.

"Emelia. What were you doing in here? I knocked on the door and you wouldn't answer me." Jasper, the pompous putz, stood with his hands behind his back like a soldier at ease. I'd never seen him do that. I'd learned in my senior year psychology class it was a display of fearlessness, superiority, as well as confidence in themselves. He knelt down and leaned in to my ear. "What did you take? If I knew you were into that sort of thing, I would have partied with you."

Omigod! He *really* is a jackass. "You pounded on my door!" I fisted my hands into the air. "And screamed my name! What are you doing here, anyways?" Anger that had long been tamped deep down into my psyche rose into my voice.

Jasper stood back and resumed his at ease stance. Muffin walked up to him, hissed, and ran out of the room. "I did not. I was knocking. I said *Emelia* a couple of times to get your attention, but it seems like you were passed out drunk on the floor." His smirk made me want to smack him in the face. I took a deep breath, ready to lash out at him, but Alexis beat me to it.

"I heard you screaming at her and pounding on her door, you freaking liar!" Alexis stood between Jasper and me, hands akimbo, her foot tapping on the hardwood floor. "I told *you* to get out and you gave me the finger. What are you doing here anyways? Nobody wants you here." Jasper shrunk back against the wall, like a cockroach when the lights come on, as Alexis called him out. He'd never seen her full on rage. I had. It was not a pretty sight. "Phillip told you to leave, and you still persist on staying here, barging into Emelia's room, and accusing her of being drunk? What the hell is wrong with you loser?" She was in his face now. I stayed where I was on the floor and enjoyed the show.

"I didn't *do* that! I was trying to help. I just wanted to talk to her." Jasper pointed to where I sat leaned against my bed. I smiled like the Cheshire cat in Alice in Wonderland. Karma was sweet from where I sat.

"Didn't you break up with her?" Alexis was a cat with a mouse. She played with him and batted words at him so quick, he didn't have time to recover, recoil, or retreat.

"No. We didn't break up."

"You broke up with me, Jasper."

"I did *not!*" Jasper was grasping now and I knew it, which made the moment even sweeter. "Just because I don't call you every day... god! You're so needy!"

"Hmm, and you're the one standing in *my* bedroom because why exactly?" I rubbed my chin. "Oh yeah, because I didn't run to the phone when you called."

"Okay. I've heard enough." Phillip crossed his arms over his chest. "Jasper, you've been asked to leave. If you don't go now..."

"You'll get your baseball bat?" I interrupted.

Phillip looked at me, a slow grin played across his lips. "Yeah. That would be quicker than calling the police." His eyes twinkled with youth. I imagined he enjoyed the thought of using Jasper's head for batting practice as much as I did.

"You'll regret this." Jasper spoke with venom on his lips. His tongue came to a point and it reminded me of a snake's tongue. "No one will ever love you like I do. You're making a big mistake, ending something so great. I want you to be happy, and I want to be the one to make you happy

"So, now you love me?" I asked. "Since when?"

"Since always." Tears welled in his eyes and I struggled not to laugh.

Such a faker. I was in my present, but I'd lived this moment in another lifetime. I wasn't as soft-hearted as I'd been before I time travelled. "Hmm. I remember you telling me you couldn't tell me you love me because I'd expect more from you. That all you had to give was what you're offering right now." I stood, a bit wobbly. Alexis and Phillip each supported one of my arms. Their eyes were fixed on me as they waited to hear what I'd say next. "If no one will ever love me the way you do," I put my hands to my throat and made gagging sounds. "Gag! I will do without love. Besides, I know I'm lovable. And more importantly, I know *how* to love others. Not just myself."

"Hey sis, I love ya." Alexis squeezed my arm.

"I love you too, Emelia." Andrea ducked under Jasper's outstretched arms and hugged me around the waist. "I'm proud of you." She whispered.

Phillip stood between us three sisters and Jasper. "Don't bother my girls again. You can leave standing, or I can drag you out of here by that mop top of yours."

The three of us giggled because none of us had heard Phillip speak like that. To anyone.

Jasper crossed his arms and stared down Phillip. My heart started to pound. Jasper had always gone on and on about his mixed martial arts training and how he didn't want to fight anyone because he knew he would kill them. I tugged at Phillips sleeve, but he didn't pay any attention. Instead, he jump footed forward. Jasper's pupils dilated, his jaw dropped, and he took off like a rocket.

We laughed as he ran down the stairs, lost his footing, and swore as he hit the floor at the bottom of the stairs. I guess because I felt vindicated at last, I went to the top of the stairs and laughed at Jasper while he scrambled to his feet. "You're all crazy." And out the front door he went, into his scrunched front end of a Nova, and burned rubber as he tore away from the curb.

Phillip put an arm around me. "Emelia, what did you ever see in that guy?" He ruffled my hair.

I leaned into his hug. "I guess I was too young or too stupid to know better."

"Emelia, you're not stupid. Young, yes." He squeezed my shoulders. "You're growing into a strong woman who makes good decisions. Like the way you stood up to Jasper. I've been waiting for you to do that."

"You have?"

"We all have." Mom joined us at the top of the stairs.

"Why didn't any of you say anything?" I looked to each one of them.

"Would you have listened? We never hid how we felt about him."

Phillip and my sisters both nodded agreement.

I sighed. "Probably not. But Mom? Where did you come from? I didn't know you were home."

She smiled. "I was getting the baseball bat."

29

Back To Reality

Life calmed down the next day. I got up early and took a long, hot bath. It was luxurious to soak in the bubbles created by my Avon pink bubble bath. The sound of my sisters laughing in their room and playing *Journey* music was the perfect medicine. I continued to wonder if everything I'd been through with Henry was real or a dream.

Maybe this would be the book I'd write.

I wished it had all been real. I just fell and bumped my head and went into some weird dream state. I sighed at the memory of Henry's kisses and his words to me at the fair. He'd tried to tell me something about college before I blipped back home. Or back awake. Everything was still processing.

I checked the back pocket of my jeans. The time twister necklace was still there.

My room was colder than usual. I looked out my window to see it snowed again. The snowy ground glistened the way it did when it was booger freezing cold. January and February were my least favorite months. Long, cold, and never-ending. The neighbor's dog danced on top of the snow. She tried and failed to find a place to pee without freezing her paws. She ran back inside to the warmth of her owner's home, leaving behind a yellow popsicle in the snow.

My room needed tidying and it seemed like a good day to do it. The phone rang from the kitchen and I called to my sisters to answer it. I was wrapped in a bath towel and didn't want to traipse downstairs. My sisters couldn't hear me over their music and laughter. I didn't know if Phillip or Mom were home, so I threw on a robe and went down to answer it after seven rings.

"So, how'd it go?"

"Kelli-Anne?"

"Cheeuh! Did it work?" Her voice oozed with anticipation.

"No. I bumped my head and woke up with a headache." My hand went to my forehead at the memory. "But I had a really good dream."

Kelli-Anne let out a long sigh. "Bummer. I was hoping it would work. Are you sure it was a dream?"

"Pretty sure. Things that good don't happen to me, ya know?"

"Aw, I'm sorry Emelia. Things will get better."

"Already have. I got rid of Jasper for good."

"About time!"

"Why am I just learning my family and best-friend hated my boyfriend?"

"We never hid our feelings about him. And I told you his temper scared me. But love blinded your perspective. You couldn't hear, really *hear*, anything we said."

"Apparently."

"So, what are you going to do about Henry?"

"I'm going to call the colleges again, just in case my dream wasn't a dream. I mean, a gypsy who can grant wishes with an ancient pendant? I was hoping. Or maybe avoiding the truth I didn't want to see."

"But... you see it now, right?"

"Yah! Of course. Never going back down that road again. In fact, I might apply to the community college and see what they have to offer in the way of work-study programs. I have my job at Fly Buyz, too. I talked to Mom and Phillip and they are willing to let me continue living at home while I go to college. That will help with expenses."

"Maybe we'll have a couple classes together."

"You have a head start on me. I'm already a semester behind, but I called this morning and made an appointment for tomorrow so I can get enrolled and the application process started."

"You've made the right choice. Good for you." Kelli-Anne stopped for a beat and asked, "So, what was the dream like?"

"Kelli-Anne, I didn't want to wake up. When Henry tried to kiss me at graduation, I let him. How did I never know what a good thing I had right under my nose all along? Why did I ever let him go?"

"Who knows why things happen the way they do. You can't be down on yourself about it. Besides, there's always hope. He may come back. If he really liked you, he won't forget about you easily."

"I hurt him, Kelli-Anne. He will never come back here. His parents moved away, so what does he have to come back for?"

"You."

"Maybe. Well, I'm in my robe, so I'll let you go so I can get dressed. I'm going to call the colleges today, for my own sanity."

"Let me know how that goes, okay?"

"Definitely. And thanks for being a part of this time-travel stuff. I'd think I was going crazy if I didn't have you to talk to about it."

"That's what friends do. Love ya, Emelia."

I went upstairs to dress for the day. While I cleaned my room, I caught sight of something that glimmered from under my bed. "What's that?" I bent to pull it out and have a better look at it. My hands trembled. It was the locket Henry bought me at the county fair. It must have snapped off when I returned from the past. The clasp had broken off. Nothing a pair of tweezers couldn't fix. I pulled my tweezers from my

makeup bag and put the clasp back together. I pinched it
shut tight and placed it on my neck where it belonged.

Maybe it hadn't been a dream after all.

30

Second Chances

The same lady I spoke with a while ago assured me Henry Fitch hadn't showed to register for classes. All I had was a dream to write about, to look back on, and remember. It could make a great romance novel. With my journalism classes, I could sharpen the rough spots and maybe make it salable.

I got my classes lined up with the help of the admissions office. The lady in the registrar's office gave me all the paperwork she could think of for every work study program, scholarship, and grant. I would start at the end of the month. So it seemed things were looking up, as Kelli-Anne had promised.

While I was totally over Jasper, my heart still ached for Henry. The gypsy lady had given me a gift and the pendant had served a purpose. In my search to find Henry, I'd found myself. I was where I needed to be right now, learning to be a strong, independent woman who would never again let a man limit what or who I could be. It was a good feeling to be in control of my own destiny, rather than waiting for destiny to happen. Better than allowing myself to be controlled by someone else's temper. And it had been in front of me all along, like Henry had. I would never let another opportunity slip through my fingers. My world was what I made of it.

Phillip drove me to school each day and picked me up after my last class. That way, I was able to use the money I'd saved for a car to pay for college. Poor Phillip had become the family chauffeur since his retirement.

I hung out in between classes in the commons room doing homework. Sometimes Kelli-Anne had a free period and we'd grab something from the cafeteria and chat over lunch. She'd broken up with what's his name. Yeah, already forgotten. I'd made a couple of friends from my classes and we worked on homework together sometimes. Other days I chilled, too tired to keep my eyes open from studying late the night before.

It was a day late in January and I had a lot of reading assignments. I passed on lunch with Kelli-Anne to get some of it done so I wouldn't be up all night. Tired and eyes half-closed, I trudged to the parking lot where Phillip picked me up. We were in the middle of a January thaw. Although a little late, it was great to have the break from the sub-zero temps we'd experienced this winter. I stood at the entrance, surrounded by the hues of dusk, and scanned the parking lot for Phillip. I didn't see the station wagon or my mom's Volkswagen. A couple of young men brushed by me and stopped briefly to ask if I needed a ride. I recognized the taller blond from my sociology class.

"No, I'm fine. My ride will be here." Phillip never failed to show. Ever. My dad had left me numerous times to stand outside of the library, the school, the mall, the movie theatre. The theme was the same. When Mom found out he'd left me for hours waiting for a ride, often in the dark, she'd ripped into him.

"Are you sure?" The blond whose name I didn't care to remember waved off his friend to stay behind and talk to me.

"I'm sure. My step-dad always shows. He might have had to pick up my sister and could be running a bit late."

He placed his hand on my shoulder. "I don't mind. Maybe we could grab some coffee. Work on our sociology homework together. I noticed you're a quick study with all that stuff. I wouldn't mind the help."

I wasn't interested in the implications a coffee date held. "I don't mind helping you sometime during one of my class breaks. Tonight, I have a lot of reading to do, so I'll have to pass. But thanks anyways."

He nodded. "Sure. Whatever. See ya." He walked away just as another man approached. He wore a uniform of blue trousers and an overcoat. His shirt was a lighter shade of blue than his coat. His hair was trimmed short. I noticed he was quite attractive. I assumed he must be a recruiter. I'd seen the Army and Navy recruiters on campus several times. This guy looked younger than the other men I'd seen. Closer to my age.

As he approached, my tired eyes registered a familiar smile and eyes I would know anywhere. My voice caught in my throat as I mouthed his name.

Henry.

I closed my eyes, shook my head, and opened again to see Henry stood right in front of me.

"Emelia." He smiled down at me. He must have grown half a foot since I last saw him.

"Henry?" I touched a brass button on his jacket to see if he was real. "Is it really you?"

He placed his hand upon mine. "It's really me, Emelia."

Omigod! I wanted to hug him. To kiss him. I leaned in, but the Henry from my life had not been kissed by me. Ever. I'd turned my head when he'd tried. "What are you doing here? What are you wearing?" I looked him over. He was beautiful. His hair perfectly combed, his eyes melty chocolate, and his perfectly plump lips begged me to kiss them. I opted for a friendly hug.

"I stopped by your house. Phillip told me where you were. I offered to pick you up and surprise you." Henry tucked my hair behind my ear and rubbed my shivering arms. "Can we talk in the car? It's pretty cold standing out here."

I nodded and followed him to his car. Did I activate the pendant in my pocket somehow? Would I awaken in my bedroom? "You look so different, Henry."

His gaze locked with mine. "So do you, Emelia. You've changed. And you're going to college." He tilted his hat from his forehead. "I'm so happy for you."

"It was a bit of a shock to me too, but I found a way to make it happen. But you..." Sadness washed over me. "You didn't go to college, did you?"

Henry shook his head. "I knew I would never go."

"But all those times we talked about it."

"I know. I really thought I'd be able to make a way, but I couldn't save enough money and my parents didn't have any." His Adams apple bobbled. "The money I did have put away, well, it disappeared from the cigar box under my bed. The day of graduation, my parents told me they were moving west and I'd be on my own. They told me I was eighteen, so I had to move out."

I laid a hand on his cheek and he leaned into it. It was a familiar motion I did automatically. "Henry... " I wanted to comfort him.

"I didn't have the heart to tell you. I was... embarrassed. The Air Force had a great opportunity for me, so the day after graduation, I enlisted and went off to basic." He took my hands in his. "I knew I'd be on my own, one way or another, with my parents moving away and leaving me behind. That's why I told you how I felt that day. Looking back, it wasn't fair of me to just dump it all on you like that." He took a deep breath. "The Air Force was only my second choice. You were my first."

My familiar foe, guilt, rushed through me. "Henry, why didn't you tell me about your parents and college? You're my best friend. Why didn't you at least write to me?"

"Like I told you, I was embarrassed Emelia." He looked into my eyes, all the seriousness of a preacher on Sunday. "I wanted to give you so much, but what could I offer you, homeless and broke?"

"Henry," I leaned closer to him. "I never cared about those things." I fought back the tears that wanted to fall. "I cared about you and you were gone. You disappeared from my life without a word of where you'd be going. I should be angry with you." I looked into his eyes. "But all I feel is joy you're here right now." I hugged him. I loved the familiar smell of him, peppermint and woodsy.

"I'm sorry, Emelia," he whispered against my head. "I should have known better. You're right. But I was ashamed."

His face was inches from mine. "You have nothing to be ashamed of Henry Fitch. You are doing an honorable thing and I'm proud of you." The words were barely above a whisper.

He sat taller in his seat. "I have a three-day leave before I have to go back." He ran his finger along my jawline. "I kept dreaming you were looking for me. And I met a woman in the cafeteria at technical school during lunch break one day. She sat down next to me and started talking about her son she was visiting. Actually, she knew you."

"Me? What was her name?"

"She didn't say, and I didn't think to ask. She only told me I shouldn't have run off like I did without telling you." He chuckled. "She told me to suck it up and stop feeling sorry for myself and make things right with you."

"Did this woman have long, dark, wavy hair and eyes like a cerulean sky?"

"Yeah. You know her?"

The gypsy woman. Could it be? No. "I met her once or twice. I'm surprised she showed up at your base."

"Well, she hit a nerve. And coupled with the dreams of you searching for me, I had to take a short leave and come back to see you and talk to you, face to face."

I leaned against his chest and burrowed into his neck. I placed kisses there and along his jawline. I placed my hand on his chest and pressed it to his heart. He tensed beneath my touch. How stupid of me! Henry probably had a girlfriend by now. It wasn't like he'd sat around and waited for me. "I'm sorry, Henry. I shouldn't have done that."

"Jasper. I remember."

"No Jasper. We're done. We've been done for a while. I shouldn't have assumed you'd be single. I'm sorry."

"No girlfriend." Henry turned up the radio. "I like this song." *Open Arms* by *Journey* played thru the static on the AM radio station. He looked at me and rubbed my shivering arms. "I went on a couple dates with some girls who hung around the base, but I couldn't give them what they wanted."

"What did they want, Henry?" I nudged him playfully and he laughed. It was like old times all over again.

"Not what you're thinking, dirty-minded girl. Well, maybe they did. I'm not a fortune teller." He ran a hand through my hair, down to my neck and pulled me to him. "My heart. It's always belonged to you."

It never happens you get to have a first kiss twice with someone you love. I was lucky enough to have that chance.

ACKNOWLEDGEMENTS

Books are a work of love and commitment and cannot be created alone.

Many thanks to my critique partner, Crystal Gross, whose insights and questions made the story stronger. She was never afraid to ask the tough questions and make me dig deeper.

Thank you to my Beta readers from Leann's Literary Lounge: Leslie Bailey, Crystal Gross, Kathleen L. Maher, and Terri Olson. You are the BEST Beta readers! Your encouragement and insights made me sharpen my pencil and give you all the best story I could.

Thank you to my editor, Cody Austin, who gave this book its final wings so it could leave the nest and fly off into the world.

Thanks to all the fantastic musical artists of the 80s mentioned in this book. Your music lent inspiration and a wonderful backdrop to many scenes.

Thank you to children's authors everywhere. You made my childhood better and kept me company on sleepless nights. You are the ones who inspired me to be a writer.

Thank you to Mr. Widen, my fifth grade teacher, who read to our class everyday from some of the greatest classics like *Where the Red Fern Grows* and *Snow Treasure*. I love books because of you.

Mostly, thank you to God for giving me this wonderful and exasperating gift. With You, all things are possible.

Dear Reader,

Narcissistic people don't just like to look at themselves in mirrors like in mythology stories or take a dozen selfies for social media sites every day. They are real monsters people battle everyday. The crazy making, the gaslighting, the intimidation and bullying are enough to make the victim feel unsure of themself and as though they are going crazy.

Until recent years, narcissistic abuse was not well known or understood. Victims had no clue what was going on and had nowhere to turn for answers or for help. Many women and men live with abuse, like mentioned in this story, believing it is their fault they are abused. Victims are ashamed and afraid to speak out about what they live with on a daily basis.

Today more is known about Narcissistic Personality Disorder (NPD) but narcissists still prey on helpless victims, generally kind women who don't set boundaries. Abuse isn't just physical it is also verbal, emotional, spiritual, medical, or financial. The bruises don't show, but the scars exist.

Finding Henry is a fictionalized story with a heroine who doesn't battle vampires or a billionaire sadist. She battles a different kind of monster, an insidious one that tries to destroy her very soul. A monster who disguises himself as an angel of light.

If you believe you or someone you know is a victim of abuse call 1-800-799-SAFE (7233).

ABOUT THE AUTHOR

Leann earned her BBA in 2014. She completed two courses on children's writing through *The Institute of Children's Literature* and has written 20 stories for *Primary Treasure*. She recently wrote and had published her first article for *Almostanauthor.com*. Leann started to write in 2006 as a newspaper correspondent. She covered and reported on village and school board meetings in her small town and has written over a hundred newspaper articles. Leann was awarded honorable mention in *Writer's Digest 75th Annual Writing Competition* in the *Mainstream/Literary Short Story Category*. She grew up in the same hometown as Lucille Ball and shares Lucy's love of comedy. She's the mother of four fabulous children and in her spare time she reads or crochets newborn caps. You can connect with her on Facebook or Instagram. She loves to hear from her readers.

Finding Henry is her debut novel.

Made in the USA
Monee, IL
22 December 2020